D1421025

THE GRUNTS
All at Sea

Praise for *The Grunts in Trouble*

Look out for:

THE GRUNTS
TROUBLE

THE GRUNTS
IN A JAM

THE GRUNTS
ON THE RUN

Philip Ardagh

THE GRUNTS
All at Sea

Illustrated by
Axel Scheffler

nosy
crow

For the real Mimi,
a real friend

First published in the UK in 2013 by Nosy Crow Ltd
The Crow's Nest, 10a Lant Street
London, SE1 1QR, UK

Nosy Crow and associated logos are trademarks and/or registered
trademarks of Nosy Crow Ltd

Text © Philip Ardagh, 2013
Cover and inside illustrations © Axel Scheffler, 2013

The right of Philip Ardagh and Axel Scheffler to be identified as the author
and illustrator respectively of this work has been asserted by them in accordance
with the Copyright, Designs and Patents Act, 1988

1 3 5 7 9 10 8 6 4 2

A CIP catalogue record for this book is available from the British Library

Printed and bound in Finland by Bookwell

Papers used by Nosy Crow are made from wood grown
in sustainable forests.

ISBN: 978 0 85763 071 1

Check out the buzz at
www.meetthegrunts.com

CONTENTS

Chapter One
A Rude Awakening

"Argh!" cried Mr Grunt, sitting bolt upright in bed.

"What is it?" groaned a dopey Mrs Grunt, rolling away from her husband and pulling their itchy bedclothes high over her head. This uncovered Mr Grunt's knobbly feet, waking a single earwig dozing between his toes.

"Someone's stolen all the light bulbs!" Mr Grunt wailed. "We have a thief in the house!"

By "house" Mr Grunt meant the extraordinary caravan he and his father, Old

Mr Grunt, had made which was now parked up in the overgrown grounds of crumbling Bigg Manor, a very big house with very few people in it.

"We don't *have* any light bulbs, you goosegog," Mrs Grunt muttered from beneath the covers.

"Spell it!" Mr Grunt blurted out, which seemed to take both of them by surprise.

Mrs Grunt threw back the bedclothes and sat bolt upright next to him. "What?" she said.

"Spell 'goosegog'," he demanded. "New rule. We can only call each other things we can spell."

"You just made that up!" harrumphed Mrs Grunt.

"It's still a rule."

"Well, it's a stupid one."

"But a rule's a rule, whether you like it or

not, trout-bag."

"Says WHO?"
demanded Mrs Grunt.

"Says me, and I'm bigger than you and I'm wearing pyjamas," said Mr Grunt. "So what I say goes."

"Then you won't be saying much from now on, will you?" snorted Mrs Grunt.

"How d'you mean?"

"If *you* have to be able to spell it."

"HA!" said Mr Grunt.

Mrs Grunt glared at him with her bloodshot eyes, not that he could see her. "That's spelled H-A," he added helpfully.

Mrs Grunt was wishing that she knew how to spell goosegog. She was pretty sure it had lots of "g"s in it. "I'm not playing your silly game, you old boot!" she bellowed, her yellow and green teeth rattling in her impressively

3

ugly head.

"This is no time to argue," said Mr Grunt, stretching his arms out in front of him like a sleepwalker. "We've got to find out who stole all the light."

"Haven't you worked it out yet?" Mrs Grunt laughed.

"Worked *what* out?" said Mr Grunt, because he really wanted to know.

You think you know the answer, don't you, dear reader? You think the reason why Mr Grunt couldn't see is because it was the middle of the night, or something, and therefore too dark – spelled d-a-r-k – to see.

d-a-r-k

But that would make Mr Grunt an idiot, wouldn't it?

And, anyway, you would be wrong. So *there*.

"Shall I tell you why you think it's so dark, husband dearest?" said Mrs Grunt, barely able to contain her glee.

"Go on, wife," said Mr Grunt suspiciously.

"Your eyes," said Mrs Grunt.

"What about my eyes?" Mr Grunt demanded.

"They're *closed*."

Mr Grunt opened his eyes and blinked in the morning light.

"Oh yes," he said, seeming both relieved and satisfied. Then, moments later, he seemed angry again. "Why didn't you tell me before?" he demanded. "Why were you keeping it a secret from me?"

Now, Mrs Grunt could have said, "Well, you were the ninny with your eyes closed; why didn't you think of opening them?" but

what she in fact said was: "Well, you keep secrets from ME."

Mr Grunt threw back the covers on his side of the bed, swung his legs over the edge and stood up, narrowly avoiding a cluster of melons on the floor. (More about those later.)

"ARRRRRGHHHH!" he cried, like a man who'd just trodden on a stuffed hedgehog – called Sharpie – with his bare feet. (This was precisely because, gentle reader, he HAD just trodden on a stuffed hedgehog – called Sharpie – with his bare feet.)

He reached down, grabbed Sharpie in one hand – *ouch!* – and threw him/it across the crammed bedroom of their caravan with all his not inconsiderable might.

Fortunately for Mrs Grunt – because it was her turn to make breakfast – she had, moments earlier, reached for a frying pan she'd been soaking overnight in a large washing-up bowl full of water beneath the bed (to save space).

She'd just sat up again, dripping frying pan in hand, when Sharpie had come hurtling through the air in her general direction, though she wasn't the intended target. Mr Grunt had been angry with the stuffed, dead hedgehog, not with her.

Raising her hands to defend herself, she found herself to be already holding an ideal flying-hedgehog-repellent, and batted Sharpie aside with the frying pan, like a tennis player would swat aside an easy ball.

The hedgehog shot through the open bedroom window before you could say, "Look out below!"

Both Mr and Mrs Grunt watched it go in silent amazement.

The silence was broken by an "Ow!"

Mr Grunt, massaging one of his hurty, Sharpie-pricked feet, took two hops over to the window and looked out.

He saw Sack, the (former) gardener of Bigg Manor, rubbing his head. Former means "no longer", so Sack was no longer looking after the acres and acres of land surrounding the huge, crumbling house.

Mr Grunt laughed and pointed. (He loved to laugh and point at people less fortunate than himself.)

"What is it, husband?" said Mrs Grunt from the bed. She was busy drying the frying pan with a corner of the itchy blanket.

"Sharpie hit Sack!" he said.

Mrs Grunt gave a hideous grin. "Serves him right!" she said.

Mr Grunt had no idea whether she was referring to the hedgehog or the former gardener. What's more, he didn't care. He had other things on his mind.

Mrs Grunt had been right. He *did* keep secrets from her. And one such secret was a secret meeting he had to attend (in secret) later that day.

Mr Grunt found himself sitting in the middle

of a round tent – where he'd been told to sit – with light streaming down on him, like a spotlight, from a hole in the roof directly above him.

"Why can't I sit somewhere else?" he grumbled to the only other person in the tent. Although Mr Grunt was directly facing the man, who was also sitting cross-legged and on the rug, the bright sunlight made it impossible for Mr Grunt to see his face, hidden in the shadows.

He assumed that this was probably because the man must be really ugly. Not everyone could be beautiful like his Mrs Grunt.

He grinned at the thought of her, adding a worrying-looking smirk to his already worrying-looking face.

He sniffed the air with flaring nostrils. And dropped the smile.

"This tent smells," said Mr Grunt, which was true. It *did* smell (though a more polite person might have chosen not to mention it).

"The walls are made from animal skins," said the man in the shadows, his voice barely above a whisper. "They have a particular smell."

"A particularly *dreadful* smell," said Mr Grunt. He breathed in deeply, then wished that he hadn't. The smell wasn't as disgusting as Mrs Grunt's breath – few things were – but it was pretty rank, in his opinion. Considering most of his meals were made from roadkill – animals scraped off the road having been killed by traffic and left on the tarmac for a couple of days – this was a bit rich coming from him, but that's Mr Grunt for you.

"HA!" he said. (He'd recently started saying "HA!" a lot and really liked it.) His bottom was already getting numb from sitting awkwardly, so he shifted his weight around a bit. "You could do with some more furniture in this smell-trap, you know," he added.

Mr Grunt found that he'd somehow got his clothes in a bit of a tangle and, yanking his sleeveless sweater out from under his bottom, managed to knock over a small, three-legged table with his elbow.

"You could do with more furniture but not so many *silly little tables*!" he snapped.

The man in the shadows gave a little cough. One of those coughs which wasn't really a proper cough at all but more of a "shall-we-get-down-to-business?" signal. "Shall we get down to business?" he said in that whispery voice of his. (I told you.)

"Ah yes, business," said Mr Grunt.

What had brought Mr Grunt to the tent was

a message: a message that had reached him in most unusual circumstances. The week before, he'd woken up and found it pinned to his chest (well, to his pyjama jacket).

He knew at once that Mrs Grunt hadn't put it there. If it had been Mrs Grunt, she'd probably have ended up pinning *him* with the safety pin in the process. And then there was the safety pin itself. Unlike the gnarled old ones in her sewing basket, or the pair she sometimes wore as earrings – when she wasn't wearing ones

made from washers – this safety pin was new and SHINY. This was a *quality* safety pin.

Someone must have walked through the grounds of Bigg Manor, climbed into their caravan, up the stairs, stepped over their sort-of-son Sunny, sleeping on the landing, and crept into their bedroom without waking them, which was quite an achievement. All the more so when you consider that Mrs Grunt nearly *always* left Sharpie lying around, like an unintended booby trap of prickles for unsuspecting feet, and you know what trouble *that* could cause.

As for the unsigned message itself, it was written on expensive paper and – although it was in BLOCK CAPITALS – it didn't look as if it'd been written by someone losing a fight with a pen. No, this message clearly wasn't from Mrs Grunt.

In brown ink on cream-coloured paper, it asked Mr Grunt to come to Gilligan's Field at 1.00pm on Thursday, but that wasn't the part that interested Mr Grunt.

It said that he was to tell no one and to come alone, but that didn't interest him much either.

But then he came to the part where it said that there would be silver coins involved. And that *did* interest him . . .

. . . so, of course, Mr Grunt told no one – because that meant that he wouldn't have to SHARE the silver coins – and, when Thursday came, he wobbled away on his trusty, rusty bike and went to Gilligan's Field at around

about one-ish, where he came across the big, round, domed tent.

"I need you to deliver a POGI for me," said the man in the shadows, making the word rhyme with "bogey".

"Right," said Mr Grunt. He had no idea who the man was or what a POGI was but didn't want to ask in case the answer the man gave was a bit boring. He wasn't interested in the details. He was only really interested in the silver coins.

Don't get me wrong. Mr Grunt wasn't one of those people whose life was all about money.

He wasn't interested in flash cars or the latest gadgets. But Mr Grunt had plans. And these plans would be helped along with some silver coins in his (rather holey) pocket.

So if Mister Hiding-in-the-Shadows wanted him to deliver a POGI then he'd deliver a POGI. Full stop.

"There are a number of people who want to get their hands on the POGI for themselves, so it's your job to deliver him as discreetly as possible," said the man.

"*Him?*" said Mr Grunt, raising an eyebrow. "The POGI is a *him* and not an *it?*" He hadn't been paying too much attention, but enough to hear a "him" when someone said it . . . or, to be more accurate, said *"him"*.

"The POGI is a Person Of Great Importance," said the shadow man with a sigh. "That's what POGI stands for, and your

– er – *challenge* is simply to get him from A to B."

"Why can't you just put him on a bus?" said Mr Grunt. Then he remembered that he was being paid silver coins for this challenge, and he didn't want to talk himself out of a job. "I'm your man!" he blurted out, suddenly waving his arms around to show his enthusiasm. (He wasn't quite sure how arm-waving showed enthusiasm, but he was convinced that a *lack* of arm-waving would show a *lack* of enthusiasm, so wave his arms he did.)

There was a crash as he knocked something else over in the shadows.

"Good," said the man (ignoring the crash, and apparently impressed by the enthusiasm). "You are to get the POGI – alive and well – to a Mrs Bayliss by the twenty-fifth. You'll find all the information you need in here."

His hand appeared out of the shadows holding an envelope made of the same cream-coloured paper as the original message. Mr Grunt took it. "But be careful," the man continued. "Let me repeat, there are people who know that the POGI will be trying to get to Mrs Bayliss and they may very well try to snatch him . . . or worse."

"Worse?" asked Mr Grunt.

The man gave another of his little non-cough coughs. "These people are the kind of people who, if they can't get hold of the POGI for themselves, may very well make sure that no one else does either."

"Oh," said Mr Grunt, not too sure what that was supposed to mean. But he didn't want to ask any more questions. He was getting bored with sitting cross-legged with a numb bum and the sun in his eyes. He *really* wanted to go.

Now the man in the shadows held out a second envelope. "This contains a photograph of the first half of the silver coins we promised you, plus some extra cash – in notes – for expenses," he said. (Now, you and I know that there's a big difference between a *photograph* of lots of money and *actual* lots of money but – then again – there's a big difference between Mr Grunt and you and me.)

Mr Grunt took it gratefully in his grubby hands. "Right," he said. "I'll be off then." He struggled to his feet and walked over to the door – a flap in the tent – then stopped, turning back to face his shadowy employer. He thought he'd better say something upbeat and positive. "The smell," he said.

"Yes?" said the shadow man.

"You get used to it after a while."

"Yes," said the shadow man. "I suppose you do."

Mr Grunt lifted the flap and went outside. He strode across the grass towards the five-bar gate his bike was leaning against, busily stuffing the two envelopes into the waist of his trousers, held up by two belts sewn together.

He climbed back on his trusty, rusty bike and was just about to pedal home . . . when a small person waddled into his path. *Waddled* because he was wearing an upturned barrel over his head and body. All Mr Grunt could see of him were his arms sticking through a hole cut either side, and his legs and feet sticking out of the bottom.

You or I might have gasped at such a strange sight. Or raised an eyebrow, or thought, "Gosh!" Mr Grunt, on the other hand, hardly seemed surprised that the guy was WEARING A BARREL.

"You're the POGI?" Mr Grunt asked.

"POGI," the POGI replied.

It must be some kind of disguise, thought Mr Grunt.

He looked at the POGI and then at the front of his bike, then at the POGI again. He pointed to the handlebars. "Jump on," he said.

The POGI struggled up on to the bike, gripping the handlebars, and dangling his legs either side of the front wheel. Mr Grunt leaned to his left, to see past the barrel, and began to pedal.

Chapter Two.

"Duck!"

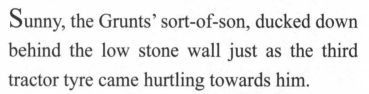

Sunny, the Grunts' sort-of-son, ducked down behind the low stone wall just as the third tractor tyre came hurtling towards him.

"Run!" he shouted.

"That's what I *am* doing!" shouted Mimi, who was indeed running, her pink-bowed hair streaming out behind her.

Hot on her heels, Sunny breathed in her vapour trail of home-made perfume, which somehow smelled as pink as her clothes and her pink-framed, pink-tinted glasses.

Just then, another tyre arced through the air and landed near their sprinting feet, a little too close for comfort. It bounced once, rolled a short distance in a wobbly zigzag, then fell sideways into a bush like a dead deer suddenly keeling over (if deer were rubbery and round).

"You shouldn't have made him angry!" shouted Mimi, without slowing her pace.

"I didn't *mean* to make him angry," said Sunny defensively. The blue dress he was wearing wasn't really designed for running in, and got tangled up between his legs. He tripped and fell, hitting his chin.

"Ooof!" he said, as most people would in the circumstances.

Mimi stopped, turned and bent down beside him in the overgrown grass. "Are you all right?" she asked.

Sunny sat up. "Never felt better." He sighed.

Suddenly, a pair of legs blocked his view: thick legs covered in wrinkled, laddered brown tights, leading down to a pair of feet rammed into a very grubby pair of bunny slippers.

"Hello, Mum," said Sunny, for the legs, tights and slippers all belonged to Mrs Grunt. (She wasn't actually his real mum. He'd been given to her as a present.)

"What are you doing down there?" she asked, not unkindly.

"I fell," he said.

"We upset Old Mr Grunt," Mimi began

29

to explain, just as a fourth – no, sorry, that should be a *fifth* – tractor tyre came hurtling towards them. (I almost lost count there.)

To Sunny and Mimi's amazement, Mrs Grunt somehow managed to catch the tyre in mid-air, spin it around and throw it back in the direction of Old Mr Grunt, where it had come from . . . all in one easy action.

"Weeeeeeeeeeeeeeeeeeeeeeeeeeeee!" she cried gleefully.

It wasn't exactly graceful, but it was certainly impressive.

A terrible crashing sound was followed, moments later, by a string of VERY rude words strung together to make one very long one. (If this were a cartoon, there'd be a speech bubble full of lots of stars, exclamation marks and fuming skull-and-crossbones.)

Mrs Grunt smiled, showing off her proud array of non-matching yellow and green teeth. "That should teach the old fossil a lesson," she said.

Don't forget that Old Mr Grunt wasn't Mrs Grunt's husband. *He* wasn't the Mr Grunt who'd come across Sunny as a baby, hanging from a washing line by his ears, and had brought him home as a present to her. No, *Old* Mr Grunt was *that* Mr Grunt's father.

"How did you manage to make him so angry?" asked Mrs Grunt.

"I asked him who he was knitting the scarf for," Sunny explained, getting to his feet and adjusting his blue dress. It hadn't always been his dress. It hadn't always been blue. It was one of Mrs Grunt's old dresses she'd passed on to him. She always dyed them blue because she knew that blue was the colour boys wore.

"Why did asking the silly old goat who he was knitting a scarf for make him throw tyres at you?" Mrs Grunt snorted.

"Because it's not a scarf he's knitting, Mum," Sunny explained. "It just looks very like one."

"It turns out it's a sweater for Mr Grunt, Mrs Grunt," said Mimi.

"The silly old truffle," Mrs Grunt grunted. (Old Mr Grunt had always liked making things, but had only recently turned his somewhat grubby hands to knitting.)

Mrs Grunt took a run at the low wall Sunny and Mimi had first ducked behind, and tried to jump over it. The result was inevitable. There was the noise of a Grunt hitting a wall, followed by a noisy grunt . . . and Mrs Grunt flipped *over* the wall, head first. A pair of upturned bunny-slippered feet appeared briefly in the air, before she disappeared from view. As Sunny and Mimi rushed forward to help, she pulled herself up, resting her chin on the top row of bricks.

"Silly place to put a wall," she muttered.

"HA!" came a shout.

No prizes for guessing where the "HA!"

came from. Whenever Mrs Grunt had an accident and there was a "HA!" you can bet your bald friend's hairpiece that the "HA!" was made by Mr Grunt. (No, not *Old* Mr Grunt. I mean the Mr Grunt who Mrs Grunt is married to. Please pay attention.) And, sure enough, this "HA!" was one of those.

"HA!" said Mr Grunt, wandering into view. He was being followed by two donkeys: Clip and her brother Clop. (Or Clop and his sister Clip.) These were the donkeys that used to pull the Grunts' caravan home.

When I say "caravan", I use the term loosely. It hadn't been bought brand new and gleaming from the forecourt of CARAVANS-4-U. Neither had it been built by Romany gypsies and passed down from one generation to the next; nor was it a classic model discovered old and neglected, and lovingly restored by a

caravan enthusiast.

No.

The caravan occupied by Mr Grunt, Mrs Grunt and their (stolen) son, Sunny, had – as I *know* I told you earlier – been built by Mr Grunt himself, with more than a little help from his dad (the tractor-tyre-throwing Old Mr Grunt). And they had built it together out of *stuff*. The end result usually made most sensible people run away when they saw it, especially now that it was being towed by Fingers the elephant.

Yes, that's right. Now that the Grunts had an elephant to pull their home, their donkeys, Clip and Clop, had retired. They got to see the countryside from a specially made trailer hitched up to the back of the van. Not that the Grunts spent as much time on the open road as they used to. Nowadays they spent more time in the overgrown grounds of Bigg Manor, which is precisely where they were now.

"Don't you 'HA!' at me, mister!" said Mrs Grunt. (Do you remember Mr Grunt's "HA!"?) She grabbed the nearest thing and threw it at Mr Grunt's head. Fortunately, Mrs Grunt was a rotten shot anyway, so the nearest thing in question – an old squeaky dog toy – didn't get anywhere near her intended target. "That father of yours has been throwing things at Sunny and Moomoo," she added.

"Mimi," Mimi corrected her. Since the Grunts had settled in the grounds of Bigg Manor – where Mimi used to be the boot boy before Lord Bigg was thrown in jail and his wife, Lady "La-La" Bigg, took charge – she'd spent a lot of time with Sunny. They'd become good friends, but Mrs Grunt still managed to get her name wrong. "Throwing things?" said Mr Grunt, his voice rising.

"Yes, mister. Throwing things!" said Mrs Grunt.

"But that's a disgrace, wife!" he said.

"Unacceptable!" she said.

"Unforgivable!" he said.

"Unimpeachable!" she said (not that she knew what it meant, though she guessed it

must have something to do with the fruit of the same name). She very much hoped that Mr Grunt wouldn't demand that she spell it.

"My daft old da needs to be taught that throwing things is always *wrong*!" Mr Grunt announced.

They all strode between the rhododendron bushes towards the shed that Mr and Old Mr Grunt used as a workshop. In Lord Bigg's day, the gardens had been beautifully tended by Sack the gardener, but those days were over.

The minute His Lordship was carted off by the long arm of the law, Sack had packed in his job, because he *hated* gardening. Now the once-immaculate lawns were growing wild, along with the flowers and the shrubs.

And the weeds?

The weeds were having a whale of a time.

Old Mr Grunt was lying on his back in the

long grass, his bottom still resting on a three-legged stool which had been knocked over at the same time as him. In his hand he still held two large knitting needles, from which hung a very long, thin piece of knitting. A large tractor tyre was lying on top of him.

"Your work, wife?" asked Mr Grunt, looking admiringly at Mrs Grunt.

"My work." Mrs Grunt nodded proudly.

They hugged.

Sunny and Moomoo – sorry, I mean *Mimi* – helped Old Mr Grunt to his feet.

Mr Grunt, meanwhile, had just caught sight of himself reflected in a number of old car hubcaps nailed to the side of the shed; trophies he'd picked up from the road or prised off cars. He turned this way and that to admire his own reflection. Then he rubbed his grubby hands through his hair and, satisfied, straightened up.

"Enough of this," he said. "We're off on a thingummy—"

"A thingummy?"

"A – er – whatsit. An *adventure*," said Mr Grunt. "There's important work to be done!"

Chapter Three
The Adventure Begins

Oh dear. Oh dear, oh dear. It seemed that whoever that man was in the shadows of the tent in Gilligan's Field – the one who gave Mr Grunt the task of delivering a POGI (Person of Great Importance) to a certain Mrs Bayliss – he didn't know the Grunts very well.

Asking Mr Grunt to deliver a POGI (Person of Great Importance) somewhere is a bit like asking a heap of elephant dung to turn out the light, or do a little dusting, or to buy you a pint of milk on its way back from Elephant

Dung School.

I chose the elephant-dung example for a very good reason, by the way – in the same way that I do most things – because, like the Grunts' own lives at that time, this story is sprinkled with elephant dung throughout.

Why?

You ask *why*?

What are you, some kind of nincompoop?

No, forgive me. That's no way to speak to anyone. It was just that kind of language which got Lord Bigg into even MORE trouble with the police when he was already being arrested for a whole long list of *other* things. The reason why this story is sprinkled with elephant dung is because it features Fingers the elephant, of course.

Of course.

And one of the things that elephants have

to do, in addition to eating and drinking and being all *elephanty*, is to have a poo once in a while. And the result? Elephant dung!

The first proper day of the adventure was the day after Mr Grunt had been handed his instructions, along with the photograph of the first half of his silver coins and the expenses money. That morning, Fingers towed the caravan out past the gates of Bigg Manor, lying crooked and broken in the overgrown grass next to the cracked and crumbling pillars that had once been proud gateposts.

Sunny was perched on the elephant's back, with the bright-pink Mimi sitting next to him. She had two hummingbirds (Frizzle and Twist) hovering above her head, which was quite normal (for her). Back down on the wooden driver's seat of the caravan sat the POGI in his barrel. In silence. Mimi glanced back at him now and again, waiting to be introduced.

"I like your new shoes," said Sunny.

"Thank you," said Mimi. "They used to be a muddy-brown colour. I painted them pink myself."

"I didn't know you could paint shoes," said Sunny.

"I am a girl of many talents," said Mimi with a grin.

"I mean I didn't know *anyone* could paint shoes a different colour," Sunny explained. "I didn't think it was possible."

"It is, and I have," said Mimi. "Have you any idea where we're going?"

"Going?" said Sunny. "Yes and no."

Just then, Fingers curled his trunk back over his head and out of nowhere handed Sunny an orange with the fingers-like tip of his trunk. Sunny patted him good and hard so that he'd feel it through his thick elephant hide.

"Thanks, Fingers," he said. He began to peel the fruit.

"Well?" asked the ever-so-pink Mimi.

"I just know that we're supposed to be delivering this POGI to someone called Mrs Bayliss—" (Mr Grunt had told Sunny and Mrs Grunt everything he felt they "needed to know", which wasn't much.)

"POGI?" asked Mimi (as Sunny had hoped she would).

"Person of Great Importance," said Sunny.

"And the POGI is the – er – person in the barrel?" asked Mimi, jerking her head in his general direction.

"POGI!" said the POGI.

"That's the one." Sunny nodded.

"And who's Mrs Bayliss?" Mimi asked.

Sunny shrugged, which when sitting on an elephant while peeling an orange with both hands is a tricky manoeuvre. If Mr Grunt had attempted such a thing, he'd no doubt have fallen off the elephant, on to Mrs Grunt and they would then both have rolled into an enormous patch of thistles. As it was, Sunny stayed pretty much upright, allowing for a little elephant sway. Well, a lot of elephant sway. Trying to stay upright on an elephant is a lot, *lot* harder than you might imagine.

"And where will we find this Mrs Bayliss?" asked Mimi.

"I don't know," said Sunny. "Dad did give me a list of places we'll be passing through on the way, though," he said.

"And I suppose –" Mimi dropped her voice, "– you've no idea who this POGI in a barrel is?"

"No," said Sunny. "I *think* that's the point of the barrel. So that no one will recognise him."

"Whoever he is, he must be very small, to fit so much of himself into that barrel," said Mimi.

"I was thinking that," said Sunny. "He's probably about the size of Jeremy." Sunny was referring to a very small man they knew who lived in a fibreglass tomato. (You can find out more about him in *The Grunts in Trouble*, in which he gave Mr Grunt a very impressive kick in the shins. And, yes, Mr Grunt started it, by kicking Jeremy's fibreglass-tomato home.)

"So you don't know who this POGI—"

"POGI!" said the POGI.

"– is, or who Mrs Bayliss is, or where we'll

find her?" said Mimi. "Right?"

"That's right, Mimi." Sunny nodded.

"Aren't you curious?" said Mimi. "Don't you *want* to know?"

"Of course I do," said Sunny, "but there's not a lot I can do about it."

"I suppose not," said Mimi. "But it is exciting, though, isn't it? I'm glad I got to come along too." She grinned.

"Me too!" said Sunny. "And it means that you'll also be around for Dad's birthday. I can't say I am sorry that Grandad is staying back at the manor."

"How old is your dad going to be?" asked Mimi.

Sunny shrugged. He had no idea. He didn't think Mr Grunt had any idea either. "I've bought him a box of chocolates," he said, "and hidden it in the caravan where I hope he'll never come across it, even by accident."

"Let me guess where—" said Mimi, but she didn't get the chance to because, at that moment, Sunny was hit on the back of the head with a currant bun. "Ouch!" he said.

"Too much noise!" shouted Mr Grunt (who had thrown the bun) from the front of the caravan.

"Listen to your father and do as you're told!" shouted Mrs Grunt, from an upstairs window. "Make too much noise!"

"That's not what I meant, wife!" shouted Mr Grunt, twisting around to face her.

"Then say what you mean, mister!" she shouted back.

"What I mean is that you're a knapsack!"

"Fish hook!"

"Rat poison!"

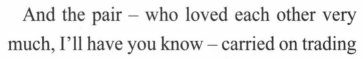

"Beanbag!"

"Gripe-water!"

"Stingray!"

And the pair – who loved each other very much, I'll have you know – carried on trading insults for the next fifty-two or so minutes it took them to reach The Happy Pig.

The Happy Pig was not a pig (happy or otherwise), though it may very well have been named after one. The Happy Pig was what's known as a tavern, and it was owned by none other than Lady "La-La" Bigg (though it was run by a man called Peach).

Yes, of *course*, this was the same Lady "La-La" Bigg who lived in Bigg Manor and had a pet pig called Poppet. And Peach was none other than the Bigg family's one-time butler. Now he no longer buttled but ran The Happy Pig for Her Ladyship instead. He loved his work, as long as Mr and Mrs Grunt didn't pop by. (The happy pig painted on The Happy Pig sign wasn't based on Poppet but did look *very* happy indeed.)

The reason the Grunts had stopped at The Happy Pig was because Mrs Grunt had wailed the word "Stop!" with such upset in her wailing that Sunny knew it was serious. If Mr Grunt had been kidnapped in the night by bad-faeries-with-attitude, for example, she wouldn't have made such a fuss. *This* wailing must be to do with one of her not-quite-pets pets.

And how right he was. Somehow, Mrs Grunt had managed to drop her old cat-shaped doorstop, Ginger Biscuit, from an upstairs window, causing his tail to become wedged between the spokes of one of the wheels . . . so now Sunny asked Fingers to stop.

And he did.

Dead in his tracks.

And, if you know anything about forward momentum – and if you don't, you might actually learn something – you'll be able to guess what happened next. Just because the elephant had stopped dead, it didn't mean the house that he was attached to stopped dead too.

No. That kept on moving and then stopped with a sudden jolt.

Mr Grunt found himself flying through the air and hitting the caravan wall or, to be more precise, a portrait on the wall or, to be EVEN MORE precise, a portrait of Mrs Grunt's particularly ugly cousin Eva who used to come out only at night to work in an observatory.

Mr Grunt was seeing stars.

Chapter Four
The Pain! The Pain!

Mr Grunt was grumpy and in pain, but not in that order. First and foremost he was in pain. Smacking into a portrait hanging on the wall of a caravan can do that to you. And it was the pain that made him grumpy. It made him SO grumpy that he wanted to kick something.

And that some*thing* almost turned out to be a some*one* because, just as Mr Grunt swung his foot at the door (because he knew it would make a satisfying sound as it rattled on its non-matching, poorly hung hinges), Sunny opened it and stepped into the room.

Having heard the terrible crashing noise Mr Grunt had made as he slammed into the portrait, the boy had slid down off the back of Fingers, and hurried into the caravan to check if he was OK. Unfortunately, he arrived just in time for the big kick.

Fortunately there was a "fortunately" as well as an "unfortunately". Because both Mr Grunt AND Mrs Grunt seemed to spend half their lives falling over, out of, into and under things (just think of the low wall on the previous day), Sunny was used to giving first aid. And recent experience had taught him that Mr Grunt found nothing more soothing on a wound – whether it was a bump on the head or a throbbing knee – than rubbing it with the cool, fleshy end of half a melon. It was for this reason that Sunny had taken to keeping a stack of melons in the kitchen of their mobile home. (I did mention the melons earlier. Look back at page 7, if you don't believe me.)

Sunny tried to keep them in a neat pile but, with the movement of the caravan and the fact that Mr Grunt regularly threw them at Mrs Grunt for fun, and Mrs Grunt regularly threw them at Mr Grunt for fun, they could usually be found rolling around on the floor (even the *bedroom* floor, remember).

Sunny, with Mimi close behind, had snatched up one of these melons as soon as he'd dashed into the caravan. When he threw open the door and Mr Grunt's big boot came into view, it was the melon in Sunny's arms that was on the receiving end.

It exploded in an impressive spray of melony pulp – along with a very squelchy noise – leaving Sunny's blue dress so splattered that he looked as if he'd been sneezed on by someone with a VERY big nose.

"Sorry," said Mr Grunt.

"That's OK, Dad," said Sunny, spitting a melon seed from his mouth and pulling another three from his ear.

"*Dad?* What do you mean, 'Dad'?" said Mr Grunt. He looked first at Sunny and then at Mimi and then back at Sunny again. "Who's driving this thing?" he asked.

"We've stopped, remember?" said Sunny. "Ginger Biscuit got caught in the spokes."

"A ginger what?" muttered Mr Grunt. "Where are we?"

"Outside The Happy Pig," said Mimi, peering out of the window at the pub sign. She liked the picture on the sign because the particularly happy-looking pig was so *pink* that it made her want to smile (so she did).

"Then we'd better camp here for the night!" said Mr Grunt.

"But we've only just left Bigg Manor, Dad,"

said Sunny.

"And it's the middle of the morning, Mr Grunt," Mimi added politely.

"Don't argue!" said Mrs Grunt, who'd just entered the room. "The idiot is always right." She had Ginger Biscuit under her arm. The cat-shaped doorstop didn't seem any the worse for wear.

"Who the blazes are you?" demanded Mr Grunt, scowling at his wife, with a strange look in his eyes.

"Who do you think I am?" she demanded. "The President of –" She paused while she frantically tried to think of a place with a president. "The President of Cheese!"

"Someone get this . . . this *billabong* out of my house!" said Mr Grunt.

"This is my house too," snapped Mrs Grunt.

Mr Grunt peered at her more closely this

time. He genuinely seemed not to recognise her. The bonk on his head had clearly affected his memory.

Just then, the POGI waddled through the doorway, to see what the fuss was all about. "POGI?" he asked.

"Eek!" cried Mr Grunt, jumping up on to a chair. "Get that thing away from me!"

In one swift movement, Mrs Grunt grabbed the POGI by his barrel and turned him around. He waddled through the doorway, back the way he came.

Mr Grunt, meanwhile, jumped down off the chair, grabbed a broom and tried sweeping his wife out of the room after him. "Dustball!" he muttered.

"Narwhal!" cried Mrs Grunt.

"Blemish!"

"Toucan-breath!"

"Earmuff!"

Mrs Grunt gasped. "Earmuff?" she said.

Mr Grunt prodded her in the tummy with the sweepy end of the broom. "Earmuff!" he repeated emphatically, with a nod of the head.

Mrs Grunt desperately tried to think of an equally offensive response. "Lamppost!" she bellowed.

A sudden look of recognition appeared on Mr Grunt's face. It was the kind of look that said, "I know you! How on earth could I forget?"

"Wife!" he cried, throwing the broom aside – which Sunny caught without even meaning to – and throwing his arms around Mrs Grunt.

"Mister!" cried Mrs Grunt, throwing her arms as far as they would go around *him*.

She gave Mr Grunt such a big kiss on the cheek that they could all hear her jumble of green and yellow teeth rattling inside her mouth.

Mimi felt a little queasy.

Sunny turned away. There are few things more embarrassing than watching your parents kiss, even if they're not your actual parents but just ones who took you from a washing line as a baby.

"Shall we get going?" Mr Grunt asked, once all the lovey-dovey stuff was over. "We have a POGI to deliver."

"Let's throw stuff at the pig sign first," said Mrs Grunt, plunging her hands into the pockets of her dress and pulling out a fistful of nuts (as in "and bolts") in one hand and a fistful of nuts (as in "to feed the elephant") in the other.

"Yeah, let's!" said Mr Grunt, and a HUGE grin spread across his grubby face. He was

clearly back to normal.
(Well, normal for *him*,
that is.)

The Grunts dashed for the
door at the same time with such
eagerness that they became wedged in the
doorway, until Mrs Grunt elbowed herself
free and made it out first.

Sunny and Mimi could
hear the rat-a-tat-
tat of both kinds
of nuts missing their
target and hitting anything and
everything but the sign. When they
too had made it out of the caravan, they
found a very angry-looking Peach holding a
tray of broken glasses in one hand, orange juice
dribbling over the sides. He was removing a
peanut from his hair.

"His fault," said Mrs Grunt, pointing at Mr Grunt.

"She made me do it," said Mr Grunt.

"Sorry, Peach," said Mimi.

"Yes. Sorry," added Sunny.

Peach looked at the children. "Not *your* fault," he said stiffly, before turning and going back inside.

A couple, who'd been about to be served their drinks at one of the small tables in front of the pub, slowly emerged from under their table. Sunny hadn't noticed them before.

"Is it over?" asked a rather nervous-looking man, with an equally nervous-looking jet-black moustache. "Have you stopped throwing things?"

"Yes, they have," said Sunny firmly.

"I was aiming at the sign," said Mr Grunt. "Anyway, you shouldn't have got in the way."

"I see," said the woman. She too smiled nervously. "Is . . . Is that your elephant?"

"He's mine," said Sunny.

"Very handsome," said the woman. She picked up the chair she'd knocked over when she'd dived for cover.

"He is, isn't he?" said Sunny proudly.

Now they were out of ammunition and the fun was over, Mr Grunt was already shuffling back towards the caravan, with Mrs Grunt (and Ginger Biscuit) just a few paces behind.

"Lovely," said the black-moustached man. It was a moustache that any walrus would have been proud to own. The man was wearing knee-length shorts and a short-sleeved, blue-and-white checked shirt. He had the hairiest

69

arms and legs Sunny had seen in his life. In fact, he looked positively furry.

The woman was also small and also thin, and also in shorts but her legs weren't hairy. As for the hair on her head, it was so thin and so lank and so colourless that it looked less like hair and more like she was wearing an old dishcloth on her head.

"Are you with the circus?" she asked Sunny and Mimi.

"No," said Sunny, sounding a little surprised.

"A carnival?"

"No," said Sunny. "Why?"

"Oh," said the man, a little hurriedly. "What with the elephant and birds, and the caravan, and your –" he paused to look at Mimi's overall pinkness before turning to Sunny in his blue dress, "colourful *costumes*."

Mimi laughed. "I see," she said. "No, we're

simply with Mr and Mrs Grunt—"

"The ones who were throwing things?" asked the woman, looking a little nervous again, and tilting her head in the direction of the caravan.

Sunny nodded.

"Where are you headed?" asked the woman.

Fingers had been getting a little bored throughout this, and, seeing a few peanuts scattered here and there where the Grunts had thrown them, he began snuffling around with his trunk. He stepped forward a few paces to reach them; still attached to the caravan, it came too.

Outside The Happy Pig, they heard the muffled "UMPH!" of Mr Grunt falling over on to Mrs Grunt.

At that moment, Peach reappeared with a clean tray and a fresh supply of orange juice. The man with the moustache and the lank-haired woman sat back down at their table.

"It was nice meeting you," said Mimi, politely.

"Sorry about the nut-throwing," said Sunny.

"G'bye, Peach," said Mimi.

"Good day, Mimi. Good day, Sunny," said the ex-butler.

The man and woman raised their glasses of juice as Mimi scrambled back up on to the caravan and Sunny on to Fingers' back.

"I'm Martha, by the way," said the woman.

"And I'm Max," said the man. "Cheers!"

"Cheers!" called Sunny and Mimi.

The caravan pulled away, narrowly avoiding a woman on a red bicycle. She swerved, and her single lemon-drop earring waggled like a ripe fruit hanging from a branch.

"Sorry!" Sunny called out after her.

The lady on the bike looked back, her earring catching the light. "No worries," she said.

Now that they'd gone, there were no clues that the Grunts had ever even stopped at The Happy Pig, except for the broken glasses,

73

splodges of spilled orange juice, a smattering of nuts (of both the edible and non-edible variety) and – oh yes – a nice, fresh, gently steaming pile of elephant dung.

Max looked at Martha. Martha looked at Max. They both smiled a little tight-lipped smile as they watched the caravan go.

Chapter Five
Speedy McGinty

The Grunts' plan, if you can call it a plan, was to reach a place called Isaac's Port by nightfall on Day Four. They didn't have to worry about exactly what time they'd arrive or about finding a place to stay because, of course, they could sleep in the caravan. But they *did* have to get there.

The Grunts didn't have a map but Mr Grunt said he knew a woman who did. And going-to-the-woman-who-did's house was the first (planned) stop on their journey on Day One.

Her name was Speedy McGinty.

They were quite a sight, heading off down the country lanes because as well as the elephant at the front and the grotesquely strange thing in the middle which could be loosely termed a caravan, there was also the trailer on the back, carrying Clip and Clop (one with her ears pointing to eleven o'clock and the other with his pointing

to one o'clock). Then, of course, there was the matter of the small-man-in-a-barrel sitting up front. Apart from saying the occasional

"POGI!" he seemed to keep himself amused by quietly humming the theme tunes of old children's TV shows. (The shows were old, not the children.)

Sunny had a rough idea of the way to Speedy McGinty's house. He and Mr Grunt had discussed the route the evening before they set off. The Grunts had been sitting outside having supper. It was a warm, bright summer's evening. The POGI was sitting in their little group, with Mr Grunt using the top of his barrel to put his drinks on.

Mr Grunt looked up from the bowl of squirrel and beetle stew resting on his knees

and said, "You see that hill in the distance with a carving of a kettle cut into the side?"

"No," replied Sunny, following the direction his dad was pointing.

"Me neither," said Mrs Grunt.

"Of course you can't," Mr Grunt said, "because all those trees are in the way!" He gave a strange snort of satisfaction, as though he'd planted them there himself, just to block their view. "But you know the hill I mean?"

"Kettle Hill." Sunny nodded.

"Right," grunted Mr Grunt. "Kettle Hill. And you know how to get there?"

"By hovercraft? Hang-glider? Eel?" Mrs

Grunt suggested.

Mr Grunt had given her one of his stares, which would be enough to stun a bank-robbing raccoon. (It would be nice to have an illustration of one of those somewhere here, wouldn't it? Let's see what happens if I ask nicely.)

The author's wish is the
illustrator's command.

Perfect.

"Sorry, mister," said Mrs Grunt, turning away from Mr Grunt's withering stare. "This adventure is getting me all excited." She then whooped like an excited schoolgirl as if to prove the point.

There was an embarrassed silence, finally broken by Mr Grunt saying, "You know how to get to Kettle Hill, Sunny?"

"As if we were going to the Ridge, then going west instead of east?" Sunny asked.

"Which ridge?"

"The one on the way to Kettle Hill, Dad."

"Oh, *that* one," Mr Grunt said. "Well, head for Kettle Hill but before you get there, go to Hutton's Vale."

"Where's that?"

"Should be signposted."

"And what will we find there, Dad?"

"A woman with maps and charts," Mr Grunt

80

said. "Speedy McGinty."

"OK," Sunny replied. He was about to ask who Speedy McGinty was, when he took a spoonful of the stew and bit on something which shouldn't have been there. He pulled it out of his mouth. It was a washer on a twisted paperclip: in other words, it was one of Mrs Grunt's earrings.

"I was wondering what had happened to that," Mrs Grunt said, snatching it from him and hooking it back through her earlobe before you could say, "Watch out for the gravy!"

And that had been that. End of conversation.

Now they were heading in the direction of Kettle Hill, with Sunny and Mimi on the lookout for the signpost to Hutton's Vale. And, sure enough, there it was.

Speedy McGinty turned out to live in a bright, modern bungalow surrounded by a very pretty garden and with a mildly sloping ramp up to the front door. This was just the kind of garden that Clip and Clop loved to eat – yes, e-a-t – so Sunny double-checked that the bolt on the back of their trailer was firmly fixed in the closed position before ringing the doorbell.

The door was opened by Speedy McGinty herself. She was in a dazzling wheelchair. Much of it was coated in gleaming chrome, that more-silvery-than-silver metal that can make just about anything look really cool.

"Hello," said Sunny. "Are you – er – Speedy

McGinty?"

Ms McGinty – who was dressed in black from head to toe – grinned, showing off a set of perfect, white teeth. "Well, that's what folks call me on account of the way I can handle this." She slapped the arms of her amazing-looking wheelchair.

From her accent, Sunny guessed that she wasn't from around those parts. "Er . . . Then what should I call you?" he asked.

"You can call me Speedy," she said. "How can I help you?" She looked over his shoulder at the extraordinary caravan.

"My father – Mr Grunt – sent me."

Speedy McGinty seemed to be taking in the boy's blue dress for the first time. "You're Sunny?" she asked.

"That's me," said Sunny.

"Is he in there?" she asked, pointing at the caravan.

"Yup. And Mum."

"That . . . That sure is some . . . home," said Speedy.

"Dad has to deliver a POGI—"

"A POGI?"

"A Person of Great Importance."

"Oh," said Speedy McGinty. "Who for?"

Sunny shrugged. "He didn't say . . . but he did say that you'd have some maps and charts we could borrow—"

"Did he now?" said Speedy McGinty. She laughed.

"Oh," said Sunny. He had that sinking feeling.

"He ain't exactly lying," said Speedy McGinty. "Just presuming. He's always been that way." She held on to both wheels then leaned back in her chair, causing the front to tilt up, and she somehow swivelled it around to face the other way, all in one fluid movement, at lightning speed. "Follow me."

Sunny followed her down her narrow hallway, the walls on either side lined with

shelves absolutely covered in trophies of all shapes and sizes, glinting almost as much as her wheelchair.

"Wow!" said Sunny. "Did you use to be an athlete, Speedy?"

"Use to be?" asked Speedy McGinty. She sounded puzzled. "Oh, I see what you mean." They'd reached the room she'd been heading for and, using the same swift manoeuvre as before, she turned herself to face him. "I've been like this all of my life, Sunny." She prodded both her legs. "These are as useless as bags of walnuts. I got all these cups and gongs and gizmos without any help from these here legs."

Sunny's face reddened. "Sorry," he said.

Speedy McGinty smiled her fabulous smile again. "Nothing to be sorry about or to feel sorry for," she said. "Now, take your pick."

Sunny didn't have to ask what she meant by that because, like the hallway, the walls of the room were lined with shelves. Unlike those in the hallway, though, these were lined with hundreds – no, thousands – of neatly folded maps and charts.

"Wow!" said Sunny, a second time. "You have a lot of maps."

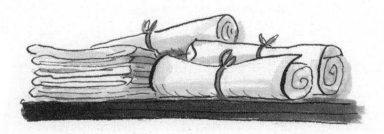

"I've been to a whole lotta places."

Sunny looked at her chair.

She laughed. "I don't go everywhere by chair, you know. I can drive just about anything on wheels . . . I can fly a plane too. But I'm real fast on this thing." She tilted back and spun herself around in her chair three times, spinning like a coin. Sunny felt dizzy just watching her.

"Lightweight aluminum frame, coated in chrome," she said. "This chair is a racer." (She said the word "aluminium" as though she'd left out a letter or two.)

"Dad needs a map to get us to Isaac's Port," Sunny explained. "And then here." He took a piece of folded-up paper out of his dress pocket and unfolded it. There were a number of place names scrawled on it in pencil, in Mr Grunt's untidy handwriting. Sunny read them out. "I don't know why he doesn't just come inside and ask you himself."

Speedy McGinty smiled. "Because he's frightened."

"What of?" asked Sunny. "Not you?"

"Not of me, no," Speedy McGinty explained. "Of the dog."

Sunny looked around the room. He couldn't see any sign of a dog anywhere.

Speedy smiled. "Look again," she said. "Her name's Petal."

So Sunny looked again, his eyes slowly scanning the room as he turned in a circle. There! This time he *did* see her. Over in the corner was a white baby-grand piano on which was a cluster of photographs in chrome frames, and curled up at the bottom of what looked like a glass, chrome-rimmed bowl was a tiny, brown-and-white dog. To call Petal "teeny weenie" would be to make her sound far bigger than she really was.

Sunny went over and peered down at her from the top. "That's Petal?" he asked.

"Sure is." Speedy McGinty grinned.

"That's the dog Dad is so frightened of?"

"The very same."

90

"Does she bite?" asked Sunny.

"No way," said Speedy McGinty, laughing. "Pick her up. Give her a hug."

A little nervously, Sunny reached his hand down into the glass. The tiny dog opened an eye and sniffed his fingers. Then she licked them.

"That tickles!" said Sunny with a smile, carefully lifting Petal out in the palm of one hand, and holding her against his chest. The dog sniffed the interesting smells on his blue dress. "She's cute," he said.

"Very," said Ms McGinty.

"So why is Dad so frightened of her?" asked Sunny. "He's not usually bothered by dogs." He had a very clear image in his mind of the time Mr Grunt had wrestled a huge German shepherd dog for a sausage that had fallen from a hot-dog van. The dog had lost.

"He was frightened he'd *tread* on her." Speedy McGinty grinned. "He thought he had once, but it turned out to be one of Petal's toys. Since then, on the few occasions he's come by on his bike to borrow things, he's always stayed out in the garden and shouted through the window."

Sunny was now studying the people in the framed photos on the piano. Speedy McGinty herself was in all of them, in her wheelchair, of course, and was shaking hands with some very famous people.

"Wow!" said Sunny, for a third time. "Is that—?"

"Sure is," said Speedy.

"And that's . . . that's—?"

"In person." Speedy nodded.

"And how come you met—?"

"I was invited to dinner."

Sunny was VERY impressed. "You must be very famous."

Speedy McGinty shrugged. "You've never heard of me," she said, and it didn't seem to bother her in the slightest.

It was true, Sunny *had* never heard of her, but there was something familiar about her, none the less.

"So how come Dad knows you?" he asked.

"This time around?" She smiled to herself. "This time around I caught him trying to prise the door knocker and door handle off the front door a few years back, to sell as scrap metal . . . and we got talking."

"Oh," said Sunny. (He didn't know what else to say.)

While they'd been talking, Speedy McGinty had been checking the place names on Mr Grunt's list, pulling various maps and charts off different shelves, and placing them on her lap. When she'd finished, she tidied them together in a bundle and passed them to Sunny.

"This is a funny-looking map," he said, lifting the folded blue one off the top.

"It's a sea chart," said Speedy McGinty.

"A *sea* chart?"

Speedy McGinty nodded. "It seems at least part of your journey to deliver this POGI of yours will have to be done by sea."

Sunny had that sinking feeling again, but it only lasted a few seconds because his thoughts were interrupted by a cry.

Sprinting to the window, Sunny saw Mr Grunt dash past as though running for his life, followed, seconds later, by a small black cloud.

It was then that Sunny and Speedy McGinty heard the humming sound. It was like the

drone of the engine of a low-flying aircraft. It was a thousand tiny buzzes buzzing as one big BUZZ . . .

"Oh no!" groaned Sunny, his head in his hands. "Bees," he said. "BEES."

Mr Grunt had a history of trouble with bees.

Chapter Six
The Man in the Motorcar

That night they camped on the roadside, and the following night, and the night after that. By the third night, the bee stings had gone down, and Mr Grunt had stopped wearing the mudpack Mrs Grunt had insisted he wear. (This was not so much to soothe the stinging as to give her something to laugh and point at.) Mr Grunt's face was left even blotchier than its usual blotchy self: a bee-scarred battlefield a few days after the soldiers had moved on.

Bee stings aside, the first three days were

uneventful. Together, Sunny and Mimi had carefully inspected the first two pages of the instructions Mr Grunt had been given, with Sunny guiding Fingers along the route they'd worked out from Speedy McGinty's maps. Then – if I've counted right – came Day Four: the day they were due in Isaac's Port. That was the day of The Unplanned Stop.

Sunny had managed to manoeuvre the hulking great caravan down a narrow hedge-lined lane – nearly being whipped off Fingers' back more than once by overhanging tree branches – when he discovered their path was blocked.

Just up ahead was a very large, very expensive-looking, open-topped motorcar. The bonnet was up, and someone was leaning into the engine from the side. All Sunny could see of him from Fingers' back was the person's

pinstripe trousers.

The person pulled his top half out from under the bonnet of the car. "Hello there!" he said. Then, taking in the odd caravan being pulled by an elephant being ridden by a wonky-eared boy in a blue dress, added, "What have we here, then?"

(Things would have seemed even more strange had the barrel-wearing POGI been sitting in his usual spot, but he was currently lying on the sofa in the Grunts' caravan sitting room.)

"Hello," said Sunny, sliding off Fingers in a

way he'd perfected after many, many months of sliding-off-an-elephant practice.

"I'm afraid the bally engine won't start," said the man. He was wearing a very dapper pinstripe suit, with a salmon-pink silk tie. He was wiping his hands – which looked perfectly clean to Sunny – on a matching salmon-pink handkerchief. He smelled of expensive aftershave.

Sunny had no idea whether "bally" was a type of car engine or not, but that didn't change the matter: the lane was blocked by a car that was going nowhere.

"Do you know much about motorcars?" asked Sunny, hopefully.

"Only how much they cost, how fast they go and which colours I like," said the man. "Why are you wearing that extraordinary dress?"

Sunny looked down at his clothes. "Er, my

mother gave it to me."

"Suits you," said the man, thrusting out his right hand. "Rodders Lasenby."

"Sorry?"

"My name. It's Rodders Lasenby."

Sunny gripped Rodders Lasenby's hand and shook it. "Sunny," he said. "I'm Sunny."

"Pleased to meet you . . . Do you deliberately have your hair like that?" Rodders Lasenby pointed at Sunny's head.

"Like what?"

"All sticking up in a complete mess?"

Instinctively, Sunny reached up and tried to flatten it.

"It just does that," he said. "I can't make it do anything else."

"Looks fantastic," said Rodders Lasenby (who had very little hair of his own except around the ears). "You don't know anything about making motorcars go, do you?"

"Sorry, no," said Sunny.

"Gosh!" said Rodders Lasenby, pointing at Sunny.

"What is it?" asked Sunny, looking around.

"Your ears!" he said. "That one's way, way, *way* higher up the side of your head than the other one."

"Er . . . yes," said Sunny. "It might have something to do with being hung from a washing line, or it—"

"Marvellous," Rodders Lasenby interrupted. "Whatever the reason, it's a great look.

Sensational. Wish mine were like that."

Mr Grunt suddenly appeared at Sunny's side. He had twigs in his hair from where he'd had to squeeze between the side of the caravan and the hedges lining the lane.

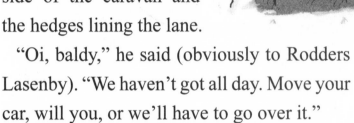

"Oi, baldy," he said (obviously to Rodders Lasenby). "We haven't got all day. Move your car, will you, or we'll have to go over it."

"Go over it?"

"You heard. Elephant, caravan, trailer and all." Mr Grunt turned and squeezed back between the hedge and van, causing some startled wood pigeons to take flight, with a loud slap of their wings.

"My dad," said Sunny.

"Sorry."

"Never apologise for your parents, Sunny," said Rodders Lasenby, walking over to Fingers and stroking him on the trunk. "One's parents are old enough to apologise for themselves. My mother was a terrible embarrassment. She used to dig her powdery hanky out of her handbag, suck the corner of it, then use it to rub imaginary dirt from my face."

"In front of your friends?"

"In front of my board of directors. Even when I became chairman of Lasenby Destructions," said Rodders Lasenby.

"Constructions?" asked Sunny, not sure that he'd heard right. He knew that "construction work" was a posh way of saying "building".

"No, *De*structions," said Rodders Lasenby. "My company specialises in destroying things . . . like my mother destroyed my confidence."

"Oh," said Sunny. "Sorry."

"Can you imagine it?" said Rodders Lasenby. "I was forty-three years old and head of a company, sitting in the biggest chair at the head of the table in the board room. . . and Mummy would toddle in and do the handbag-and-hanky routine . . . The shame."

"That *is* embarrassing," Sunny agreed. "Does she still do stuff like that?"

"Not since I locked her in the cellar!" said Rodders Lasenby with a laugh.

Sunny laughed too, but a little uneasily.

"Joke," said Rodders Lasenby. "That was a joke."

"Oh," said Sunny. "Good."

"My mother's long since dead."

"I'm sorry—"

"At least I assume she must be," said Rodders Lasenby, now mopping his forehead with the salmon-pink hanky. "I didn't leave her any food down there."

He could see a look of horror cross Sunny's face.

"Another joke!" said Rodders Lasenby, chuckling.

Mr Grunt reappeared. This time he was holding a squirrel sandwich. The dead squirrel had been roadkill, so was already conveniently flat enough to slip easily between two slices

of bread. "Still here?" he said gruffly.

Rodders Lasenby nodded. "I was wondering if your elephant—"

"Fingers," said Sunny.

"If Fingers could push me into the next turning to a field, and you could sail past in your delightful home?"

Mr Grunt chewed thoughtfully on a piece of sandwich. "Good idea!" he said. "Sunny can help."

"Thank you," said Rodders Lasenby. He eyed the bee stings on Mr Grunt's face as he climbed back into the driver's seat and waited while Sunny unhitched Fingers.

Once the pushing and shoving was over, and the vehicle was safely parked up off the lane by a five-bar gate, Sunny fed Fingers his reward.

"Good work, boy," said Sunny, giving him a currant bun, and rubbing his trunk. The elephant looked back at him with intelligent eyes, then did a big poo.

(Yes, it's dung time again. I did warn you!)

Rodders Lasenby, meanwhile, jumped out of the car and took off his jacket, revealing a very smart yellow waistcoat. He draped the jacket over the passenger seat.

"Nicely done," he said, checking the back of the car for any scratches or dents. "I don't suppose I could persuade your parents to give me a lift to the nearest town, could I?"

he asked. "Then I can arrange for a garage to come and pick up Betsy."

"Betsy?" asked Sunny, feeding Fingers his final currant bun.

Rodders Lasenby patted the motorcar. "My Betsy," he said.

"With any luck," said Sunny. "And if Mum and Dad won't let you in the caravan, you could always ride up front with me."

"Too kind," said Rodders Lasenby. "I don't deserve it, you know. I can be so *very* unpleasant."

He wasn't lying on that point, dear reader, but you might have worked that out for yourself.

The Grunts didn't seem bothered. They'd just settled down to stare at the fish tank that had taken the place of the screen in their old TV set. Mrs Grunt had propped up the ginger cat doorstop between them on the overstuffed sofa, recently vacated by the POGI. There was a bowl of strips of crispy roadkill badger-skin on the small table in front of them (which, I'm told, taste a bit like pork scratchings).

"Yes, he can come with us if you like," said Mrs Grunt.

"As long as we get moving again," said Mr Grunt. "We're in the middle of an important mission, remember."

"I remember, Dad," said Sunny. He went to give Rodders Lasenby the good news.

All this time, Mimi had been having a nap *under* the kitchen table, which was also where she slept at night, it being a one-bedroom caravan. Awake now, she emerged to see what was happening, taking the POGI by the hand. As usual, she had the two hummingbirds, Frizzle and Twist, hovering above her head. On seeing Rodders Lasenby, they behaved in a peculiar manner. A *most* peculiar manner.

They flew away.

Mimi was startled.

First, no Frizzle. Then, no Twist.

"What's up with them?" asked Sunny.

"I don't know," said Mimi, looking around for any sight or sign of the birds. "They've never done that before."

"POGI!" said the POGI.

"Perhaps they don't like my aftershave," said Rodders Lasenby. He stuck out his hand to Mimi. "Rodders Lasenby," he said.

Mimi shook it. "Mimi," she said.

"You've really overdone it with the pink, haven't you?" he said.

"I – I –"

"Pink, pink, pink, pink, PINK. Overdone. Overdone. *Overdone*," said Rodders Lasenby. "I just *love* overdone. It's how I like my steaks done . . . cooked to a crisp. Lovely."

He then thrust his hand into the POGI's. "Rodders Lasenby," he repeated. "Short for Rodney. The Rodders part, that is. Lasenby isn't short for anything."

"POGI," said the POGI.

"Why on earth would a fully grown man wear a barrel?" said Rodders Lasenby. "If you *are* fully grown, that is. You're very squat, aren't you? Very dumpy . . . Look like you've been sat upon. Marvellous. If only we could *all* look that good in wooden clothing . . .

What a fashion!"

He opened the boot of the car and pointed to an extraordinarily expensive-looking suitcase. It was of light-brown leather, with a studded gold trim. "One of you carry that for me, would you? I don't really *do* carrying."

Sunny and Mimi ended up having to carry it between them, it was so heavy.

"He's very rude, isn't he?" Mimi whispered as they lugged the luggage over to the caravan.

"I think so," said Sunny, "but I'm not sure."

"POGI!" said the POGI.

"What do you mean you're not sure?" said Mimi. "How can you be not sure?"

"Couldn't he be one of those people who other people admire for speaking their own mind? You know . . ."

"Well, he sounds rude to me," Mimi whispered.

"He said something about being the boss of a company," said Sunny. "Lasenby Destructions."

Sunny stumbled and dropped a corner of the suitcase on the road. A woman passing by on a red bike swerved to avoid it. Her single lemon-drop earring waggled like the clapper in a bell. "Sorry!" Sunny called out after her.

The lady on the bike looked back, her earring catching the light. "No worries," she said.

"Careful!" said Rodders Lasenby. He was more worried about his suitcase.

"What have you got in here?" asked Mimi. "Rocks?"

Rodders Lasenby laughed.

"There's something *strange* about him," said Mimi to Sunny under her breath. "And he certainly upset Frizzle and Twist. Animals instinctively *sense* these things, like rats

fleeing before an earthquake."

"But Fingers seems fine with him," Sunny pointed out.

"That's true," Mimi conceded. "But still, I'm going to keep an eye on Mr Lasenby. Your dad did say that he'd been told other people are after the POGI, remember."

They'd reached the front of the caravan – where Fingers was now hitched up again – and heaved the suitcase up into a space beneath the wooden bench that acted as the driver's seat.

The POGI scrambled up after it and sat back in his usual place.

Rodders Lasenby, meanwhile, had put his jacket back on and was now busy putting up the roof of the motorcar. "In case it rains," he explained. He patted his beloved vehicle. "See you soon, Betsy, old gal," he said.

He strode past Fingers, narrowly avoiding a fresh pancake of elephant dung, nodded to him in acknowledgement of a job well done, and shook him by the trunk (as though it were another hand). He jumped up on to the seat next to the POGI.

Lasenby turned to the man in the barrel.

"Hope you don't mind sharing?" he said. The POGI said nothing. "Off we go then," he said. He sounded like a man used to giving orders.

Sunny and Mimi climbed up on to Fingers.

"OK, boy," said Sunny. "Let's get a move on!"

Chapter Seven
The Wodge

Rodders Lasenby stayed with them all the way to Isaac's Port, sitting up on the wooden driver's seat at the front of the van next to the POGI, talking to Sunny and Mimi up on Fingers' back.

He commented on much of what he saw as they passed. "Did you see the flowers in that garden? Every single colour you can imagine, all clashing with each other. No thought put into planting. Just thrown together all higgledy-piggledy . . . Looks wonderful!" or

"Who on earth would build a house so close to the edge of a river? It's a health hazard. Fantastic! Such originality!" and "Did you see that woman back there with that crazy bright-green wig? So obviously nylon, and not real hair! It really brought out the colour of her eyes."

Sunny found listening to Rodders Lasenby was a bit like listening to two people with totally opposite views. Sometimes a look would pass between him and Mimi, and she'd raise an eyebrow or shrug.

Then there was the fact that they passed at least two villages and one town with a garage where they could have dropped Rodders Lasenby off to have someone go and collect Betsy, his beloved motorcar. But he insisted on staying with them.

"I don't want to inconvenience you any

further," he explained. "I've taken up too much of your time already. We'll go our separate ways when we reach wherever it is you're going."

Wherever-it-was-that-they-were-going (also known as Isaac's Port) turned out to be a very pretty little fishing village, with lanterns strung around the curved harbour wall. The tide was high and a variety of boats, from fishing smacks to yachts, bobbed around on their moorings.

The light was fading fast when they finally arrived and Sunny folded away the map, but it was still bright enough to see that the place where Mrs Grunt insisted they park up for the night was wholly unsuitable.

"I still think we should stop just outside the village, Mum," said Sunny. "There are plenty of open spaces."

"Nonsense," said Mrs Grunt. "Here's much better. Look. We even have running water to *wash* with." On the word "wash" she glared at Mr Grunt with a you-could-do-with-a-good-wash stare.

The running water she was referring to was

a great big fountain, shaped like a mermaid
with water spouting from her mouth.

"I don't wash in mermaid drool, wife," said Mr Grunt.

"You don't wash at all," said Mrs Grunt.

"Then how come I don't smell?" demanded Mr Grunt.

"You don't smell because you STINK," said Mrs Grunt.

"You're the stinking one!" said Mr Grunt. "Stinkhorn!"

"Cheese-breath—"

"There's running water here because we're in the middle of the market square, Mrs Grunt," said Mimi, boldly. "I'm sure there must be laws against us camping here."

Mr and Mrs Grunt both fell silent for a moment. They weren't used to being interrupted mid-name-calling, especially not by a child. And there was something different about her. Oh, yes. Where were those little flappy birds that were usually hovering above her head?

"I know you mean well, Moomoo—"

"Mimi," Mimi corrected Mrs Grunt.

"POGI!" said the POGI.

"I beg your pardon?" said a confused Rodders Lasenby. "None of you is making the slightest sense! What a refreshing change from my daily life! I love it! Lend me a hand, will you, please?" He'd jumped down from the wooden seat and was now trying to pull his very expensive, very heavy suitcase out from beneath it.

"I'd love to help, but I'm too lazy," said Mr Grunt.

"Here," said Sunny. "Let me."

Mimi took the other end of the suitcase and they heaved it to the cobbled ground of Isaac's Port town square.

"Bring it over here, would you?" asked Rodders Lasenby, straightening his salmon-pink tie, adjusting the salmon-pink silk kerchief in the breast pocket of his pinstripe jacket, pulling down on the bottom of his yellow waistcoat with one swift tug, and striding across the square in the direction of somewhere called O'Neill's Hotel. Sunny and Mimi half carried and half dragged the case across the cobbles, behind him.

"I'll need a place to sleep tonight," said Rodders Lasenby over his shoulder. "I can have Betsy retrieved in the morning."

The lobby of O'Neill's Hotel was small and inviting. There was a staircase made of old, dark wood to one side and a reception counter made of old, dark wood to the other. Running across the middle of the low ceiling was a very long and wide beam made of – you've guessed it – old dark wood.

There was a well-worn brass bell on the counter. Rodders Lasenby rang it.

"*Ting*," it went. "*Ting*."

A woman with blonde hair piled high into a beehive appeared through a low doorway, the other side of the counter. She was dressed in a black jacket and matching skirt with worn, shiny patches, and looked bored and tired. But when she saw Rodders Lasenby in his expensive-looking clothes, she stood to her full height and fixed a welcoming smile on her face.

"Good evening, sir," she said. "How may I

help you?"

"What a poky little lobby," he said. "So small and so dark . . . Charming! I love it . . . I'd like a room, please."

The woman – whose name badge said she was called Tammy Hoot – asked him if he'd booked one.

Rodders Lasenby shook his bald head, sending out subtle wafts of expensive aftershave in her direction.

"Alas, no, Ms Hoot," he said. "I didn't know I'd be here. Betsy broke down, you see—"

"Your good lady wife?" asked Tammy Hoot.

"My car," said Rodders Lasenby. "I'm not married."

A flicker of something – hope? opportunity? indigestion? – passed across the receptionist's face.

"Well, I'd love to help you, but I'm very

sorry, Mister –?"

"Lasenby . . . Rodders Lasenby."

"I'm very sorry, Mr Lasenby, but we don't appear to have any rooms available at the moment." Tammy Hoot was flipping through a big, red, leather-bound ledger resting on the counter.

"Oh dear," said Rodders Lasenby, not sounding in the least bit concerned at the news. "Your hairstyle is most unusual, Ms Hoot. Odd doesn't even go halfway to describing it. Most becoming. Uniquely attractive."

Tammy Hoot smiled a lovely smile.

Rodders Lasenby took out his wallet and pulled out a huge wad – I want to say "wodge", so I'm going to – a huge WODGE of notes, and held them out in front of him.

From the hotel entrance, where they were now resting with the heavy suitcase at their

feet, Sunny's and Mimi's eyes widened.

"Would you mind taking this ridiculously large sum of money for me, please, Ms Hoot? It's weighing down my wallet, and leaving an unsightly bulge in my jacket."

"But, Mr Lasenby . . ." said Tammy Hoot.

"Perhaps you'd be kind enough to spend it on yourself, too. I have so little time. You'd be doing me a real favour." Rodders Lasenby pulled himself to his full height. "Now, would you be kind enough to check again for a free room? Just in case you missed something."

Sunny and Mimi looked on with wide-eyed amazement from the doorway.

Tammy Hoot took the wodge – yes, WODGE – of banknotes and slipped them into a pocket of her black jacket. She then went through the ledger a second time, and snapped it shut.

"Oh, silly me," she said. "I'd quite forgotten.

The Portview Suite is available . . . I don't know how I missed it . . ." She was a terrible actress. "It's a lovely suite. Bedroom, separate sitting room and bathroom."

She turned, beehive hairdo bobbing, to a series of pigeon holes behind her, made of old, dark wood, and pulled out a gold key on a large maroon key-fob on which was written: "PORTVIEW" in bold, gold letters. She handed it to Rodders Lasenby.

"Would you like to go straight up to your suite?" she asked. "We can sort out the – er – paperwork later."

"Thank you," said Rodders Lasenby.

"And would you like some help with your luggage?"

At this point, Tammy Hoot noticed that Rodders Lasenby didn't appear to *have* any luggage. Then she spotted Sunny and Mimi with the suitcase at the door.

"No, I'm fine, thank you, Ms Hoot," he said. "I have two very able helpers."

And it was the two very able helpers who lugged the suitcase right to the top of O'Neill's Hotel, because that's where the Portview Suite was, and the hotel didn't appear to have a lift.

"Thank you," said Rodders Lasenby when they finally reached the door to his suite. "I can take it from here."

He dug his hand into the pocket of his pinstripe trousers and pulled out two sweets wrapped in foil. He handed one to Mimi and the other to Sunny.

"They taste extraordinary. Most strange.

Rather like old dishcloths," he said. "What could be more delicious?"

"Quite," Mimi panted.

"Absolutely," panted Sunny.

"Goodbye," said Rodders Lasenby. "Thank you for all your help."

When Sunny and Mimi had walked all the way back down the old, dark wood stairs (with aching arms) and were crossing the lobby, they overheard Tammy Hoot in conversation with a rather upset-sounding couple.

"But I booked the Portview Suite this

morning," the man protested. "I recognise your voice. It was *you* I spoke to on the phone!"

"He did!" insisted the woman. "He did."

"I'm very sorry," said Tammy Hoot, "but there appears to have been some kind of mix-up. The suite is already occupied and I can't possibly let you have it—"

Mimi tugged at Sunny's arm. "It's them," she whispered.

"Who?" said Sunny.

"*Them*," whispered Mimi. "Max and Martha. The couple we met outside The Happy Pig. The ones hiding under the table."

Sunny peered at them across the dingy lobby. "You're right!" he whispered excitedly. "Only this time, SHE'S the one with the walrus moustache! It must be *fake*!"

Chapter Eight
To the Harbour!

Early next morning, Sunny was woken by Mr Grunt who'd been woken by a trumpeting Fingers, who had, in turn, been woken by a band of angry fishermen. As usual when they were on the road, Sunny was sleeping on the landing outside Mr and Mrs Grunt's bedroom, so when Mr Grunt threw open the bedroom door and tripped over the sleeping boy, the sleeping boy became a wide-awake boy and Mr Grunt became a man tumbling down the stairs.

When Mr Grunt reached the foot of the stairs (with a crumpled "Argh!"), he stood up and fumbled for the nearest melon. Having rubbed his sleepy eyes and grunted (twice), he then broke the melon in two by hitting it against the wooden back of a kitchen chair a few times, and pulled it apart. Pressing the soothing, flesh-end of one piece against a sore elbow, he yanked open the back door of the caravan and stumbled out, blinking, into Isaac's Port's market square.

"You can't camp here!" said the largest of the fishermen, before the door had even had a chance to swing shut behind Mr Grunt. The fisherman was a real hulk of a man who seemed to be more grey beard, blue cable-knit sweater and black wellington boots than anything else.

"S'right. You tell 'im, Wellum!" muttered

a smaller version of the man. He was dressed identically to Wellum, but his beard wasn't as grey, and the tops of his wellies were turned down.

The other assembled fishermen added their support to what Wellum had just said with a variety of grunts and noises worthy of Mr Grunt himself.

"Who says we can't camp here?" Mr Grunt demanded.

"Perhaps you set down after dark," said Wellum, giving Mr Grunt the benefit of the doubt. "Perhaps you didn't realise you was camping right in the middle of our market where we sells our fish."

"*Dead* fish?" asked Mr Grunt.

"Course they's dead!" said the mini-Wellum with the turned-down boots, who went by the name of Mollusc.

"So," said Mr Grunt, plonking himself down on the top back step of the caravan, "let me get this straight. You're suggesting that *dead fish* are more important than my family and animals? More important than living, breathing me?"

"Course not," said Mollusc.

"I was goin' to ask you about the elephant," said Wellum, lifting his booted foot, the bottom of which was covered in elephant dung. (Yup, it's d-u-n-g time again.) "But first, I'm askin' you – real polite – if you'd move your . . . yourselves elsewhere. This is our fish market. There are stalls to get put up, and fish to sell."

"I see," said Mr Grunt.

"What is it, mister?" asked Mrs Grunt, sticking her head out of the top of the stable-like door. "It's too early. Come back to bed." She really wished he would. She'd stuck

Sharpie, her stuffed hedgehog, under the blankets on Mr Grunt's side and couldn't WAIT to see his reaction when he rolled over on to all those prickles.

"These people care more about their dead fish than they do about us," Mr Grunt explained over his shoulder.

Mrs Grunt seemed to think for a moment, which is almost as unusual as seeing a duck carrying an umbrella. (Almost.) "Well, we are at the seaside," she said, at last.

Mr Grunt got up off the step and turned to her. "What's that got to do with anything?" he asked.

"Well, if I lived on a toad farm, I'd probably care a lot more about toads than I do now," she said with an isn't-it-obvious tone to her voice. "Maybe it's the same for these men, living so close to the little fishes."

Mr Grunt was impressed. What Mrs Grunt was saying made perfect sense (to him, at least). He suspected he must be dreaming, so he pinched her as she came down the steps of the caravan. He knew full well that it was traditional for people to pinch *themselves* to see if they were dreaming but, just in case he *was* awake, he didn't want to hurt himself.

"OUCH!" said Mrs Grunt. "You guillemot!"

"Tumbleweed!"

"Plughole!"

"Snapdragon . . . I'm not dreaming, am I?"

"No, you're not dreaming," said Mrs Grunt.

"Thought not," said Mr Grunt. He glared at Wellum. He glared at Mollusc. He glared at all the other fishermen. "Then I suppose we'd better move, hadn't we?"

By now, Sunny had also emerged, and had been joined by Mimi. She'd been woken up by the fishermen's arrival and Fingers' trumpeting, further disturbed by Mr Grunt tripping over Sunny and falling down the stairs, and made wide awake by his breaking open a melon on the chair right by her head, before dropping the unwanted piece of the fruit splatteringly close to her head.

She helped Sunny hitch up Fingers, who seemed pleased to see her. As did Frizzle and Twist, who came humming out of the early morning sky and assumed their position hovering just above her head, their tiny wings a blur. Mimi smiled. "You're back!" she said. (She'd been worried she might never see them again when they hadn't reappeared after she'd left Rodders Lasenby back at the hotel.)

Mollusc turned to Wellum and faced his stomach. (Wellum was huge, remember.)

"This just gets weirder and weirder," he said.

"And weirder," Wellum added, thinking just two "weirder"'s didn't express just HOW weird things had become.

"Anyone seen the POGI?" asked Sunny. He let out a big yawn, and stretched.

"No," said Mimi, surprised that she'd forgotten all about him.

Sunny saw an expression of even *more* surprise on Wellum's face and followed his gaze. Across the market square strode the POGI, swinging a string bag containing what appeared to be two pints of milk and a very large selection of cheeses.

"Oh, *there* you are!" said Mimi.

The POGI said "POGI!", and gave a cheery wave.

Mimi gave a cheery wave back, causing a woman passing by on a red bike to swerve. Her single lemon-drop earring waggled like a boxer's punch-bag.

"Sorry!" Sunny called out after her.

The lady on the bike looked back, her earring

catching the light. "No worries," she said.

Mollusc sighed. "How long will you be campin' in town?"

"We're not camping," Mr Grunt interrupted.

"We're stamping!" said Mrs Grunt, stomping down the back steps in her bunny slippers. She cackled.

"Not that either, wife!" said Mr Grunt. "We'll be taking a boat along the coast." (He was a man on an adventure with a Person of Great Importance to safely deliver, remember. And soon-ish.)

"All of you?" asked Wellum, raising a very bushy eyebrow, and fixing an eye on the elephant.

"All of us," said Mr Grunt. "Where we go, the caravan goes, the elephant, the donkeys—"

"Barrel boy?" asked Mollusc.

"– and all," said Mr Grunt.

"Then you'll be needing a very big boat," said Mollusc.

"No I won't," said Mr Grunt. "HA!"

"No he won't!" said Mrs Grunt triumphantly. Then she turned to Mr Grunt. "Why not, mister?" she asked.

"Because we've already *got* a very big boat," said Mr Grunt. He fumbled in a trouser pocket and pulled out a sweet wrapper with some writing on it. (He'd gone to bed without undressing, so was fully clothed.) "*The Merry Dance*," he read aloud.

Wellum's eyes widened. "Ma Brackenbury's old tub!" he said.

There was a murmuring among the fishermen.

"It'll be big enough, I grant you that," said Wellum. "You should all fit aboard—"

"If it don't sink first!" laughed a wiry sailor at the back.

"Ignore 'im," said Mollusc. "I'll shows you where to find Ma Brackenbury."

While he led the Grunts away in the caravan, the others started setting up the market stalls with the skill and precision of those who'd carried out the task a thousand times before. There was the clank of metal poles, and the rustle of red-and-white striped awnings, as the market took shape and, in next to no time, the place was piled high with white boxes full of a rainbow array of different types of fish, packed in ice.

Watching moustachelessly from the doorway of O'Neill's Hotel were Martha and Max. Both very crumpled-looking. After their hotel suite had been "stolen" by Rodders Lasenby, they'd had to sleep in – or on – their motorbike-and-sidecar. Martha had slept, seated, in the sidecar. Max had slept – or tried to – lying on the motorbike itself. Both had found the whole experience lumpy. And, although silent, their silence spoke volumes. It was if they had invisible rays coming off them like steam. Rays which said "Angry!" and "Up to No Good!"

Sunny and Mimi had *tried* to speak to Mr and Mrs Grunt about this moustache-swapping couple the previous evening – to *warn* them – but the Grunts hadn't been in the slightest bit interested.

"So the woman is wearing the moustache

that the man was wearing when you first saw them at The Happy Pig?" asked Mr Grunt. "So what? Perhaps they take it in turns."

"There isn't a law against swapping moustaches, you know!" said Mrs Grunt, holding up Ginger Biscuit's rigid, stuffed tail to her upper lip. "It ain't illegal!"

"But they could be after the POGI!" said Sunny, a little too loudly for Mimi's comfort.

"Shhh!" said Mimi, looking around for any sign of Rodders Lasenby. She didn't trust that man one little bit.

"Aren't we supposed to be on the lookout for suspicious characters, Dad?" Sunny reminded him. "Aren't we supposed to be on our guard?"

"The only thing you're supposed to be on is that elephant!" said Mrs Grunt. "But not until the morning."

And now that morning had come. And, sure enough, Sunny was back on the back of Fingers as they made their way along the top of the right-hand curve of the harbour wall in search of *The Merry Dance*. This required some very nifty footwork from the elephant. There were the harbour waters to the left of them and the open sea to the right. One wrong move and the Grunts' home – along with the

150

Grunts themselves – could have
found itself in deep water.

A few metres from the end of the wall was a tall, thin shed, like a sentry box, so narrow that there was only enough space for one person to sit inside it and the person the Grunts found sitting inside it was an old woman, wrapped

in a tatty old octopus-patterned duvet, with a long-stemmed clay pipe sticking from her mouth. She had wispy hair of the most unnatural yellow.

Sunny slid off Fingers' back, in that really cool way of his, and coughed politely. The old woman opened one large, milky eye.

"Yeah?" she rasped.

"Are you Ma Brackenbury?" asked Sunny politely.

"Guess how many kids I've had," said the old woman, scratching her leathery, weather-beaten face with her stubby fingers.

"Three? Four?" Thirteen? Fourteen? Sunny had no idea. (How could he?)

"HA!" said the old woman loudly, which not only surprised Sunny but also Mrs Grunt who was listening from an upstairs window, and Clip and Clop seated in their special trailer.

They stopped chewing for a moment and looked up. Why? Because the old woman's "HA!" could hardly have sounded more like one of Mr Grunt's "HA!"s if she'd tried.

"I've never had a single baby in me life," she said.

"So . . . so you're not Ma Brackenbury, then?" said Sunny.

"I *am* Ma Brackenbury, but I don't want you to go thinking I'm called Ma Brackenbury simply because I'm a ma, which I ain't anyways."

"I see . . . at least, I think I do," said Sunny. "Sort of."

Ma Brackenbury sucked on her long-stemmed clay pipe. It wasn't lit, and it contained no tobacco. The old woman was simply sucking air through it. She now had both milky eyes fixed on Sunny.

"Er, then why are you called Ma?" he asked.

"Short for Marlinspike," said Ma Brackenbury.

"You're named after that thing used for separating strands of rope?" asked Mimi, who'd been sitting quietly on Fingers' back all this time.

Marlinspike Brackenbury dropped the corners of her mouth and nodded. "You come from seafarin' folk?" she asked her.

Mimi shook her head. "I read about them in a friend's magazine," she explained. The friend she referred to was another of the ex-servants still living at Bigg Manor. Her name was Agnes and she used to be Lord Bigg's cook. She was married to yet another ex-servant, Jack the Handyman, also known as Handyman Jack.

There had been a time when Sunny had thought that Agnes and Jack might be his real parents. This was mainly based on the only two memories he had of his very early childhood: his father's VERY shiny shoes, and his mother's beautiful singing voice as she sang about lambs. (And, on both counts, Agnes and Jack had fitted the bill.)

Nowadays, though, Sunny was wondering whether he might just be the son of Lord and Lady Bigg. They had lost a boy named Horace, who would have been the same age as him, and couldn't remember where they'd left him. To be honest, Sunny wasn't thrilled at the prospect that he might turn out to be the son of the oh-so-nasty Lord Bigg and the oh-so-wacky Lady Bigg, but he still wanted – *needed* – to know.

Lady Bigg didn't seemed too bothered either way. On the few occasions he'd tried to bring up the subject, she'd seemed far more interested in discussing pig pellets or nose-rings. He assumed they were for Poppet, but knowing Lady Bigg, he couldn't be sure.

Back when Lord Bigg was still master of Bigg Manor, being one of his servants had been so dull and depressing that Agnes had taken out a weekly subscription to *Dull* magazine.

Dull magazine is a weekly magazine full of such boring articles that it's supposed to make you feel better about your own sad life. It was in its pages that Mimi had once read a whole three-page article about unravelling strands of rope with a marlinspike. There had even been photographs of different types of marlinspike and some diagrams. (That was the same edition that had a pull-out guide to How Lampshades Are Made.)

"You's come for *The Merry Dance*, I take it?" said Ma Brackenbury.

"Yes we has," said Sunny. "I mean have. Yes we *have*."

As Ma Brackenbury struggled to her feet, Sunny wondered whether she would throw off her duvet to reveal a wooden leg, but that wasn't the case. She had two perfectly ordinary – if slightly bowed – legs inside a pair of worn black trousers, ending high enough above the ankles to reveal plenty of red-and-white striped sock.

She grabbed a walking stick leaning against the hut wall to support herself.

She saw Sunny looking at the fish-shaped handle.

"Scrimshaw," she said. "Carved whalebone."

Poor whale, thought Sunny.

Ma Brackenbury led them with impressive speed to the tip of the harbour and there, moored to the outer wall – the sea side – with two of the thickest ropes Sunny had ever seen, was a large, wooden boat.

It's difficult for me to describe the size of the boat because I'm not very good with feet and inches or metres. I think boats might be described in tonnage anyway. What I *can* say is that it was pretty big.

"Clinker built," said Ma Brackenbury.

"What does that mean?" asked Sunny.

"The wooden boards she's made of overlap," she said, pointing to the hull. (People often refer to boats as "her" or "she".)

"Oh," said Sunny. If they overlapped, surely that made it harder for water to seep in between the gaps and, therefore, the boat was less likely to sink . . . ? And that was a *good* thing, wasn't it?

The Merry Dance was obviously old, but she didn't look in a bad way (to Sunny's completely untrained eye). Sunny had been fearing some old rust bucket but – without being made of any metal to go rusty – that wasn't the case.

"How do we get on board, Ma?" asked Mimi, back on the elephant. "Gangplank?"

Ma Brackenbury shook her head. "Tide's going out," she said. "That boat's soon goin' to disappear behind the harbour wall." She leaned precariously over the edge. "There's an iron ladder set in the stonework." She pointed with her stick . . . the one she should have been using to help with her balance.

Sunny held his breath.

But she was fine.

"But – er – we want to take everything on board," Mimi explained.

"Does 'everything' include your big-eared friend?" asked Ma.

Mimi couldn't help glancing at Sunny, though she felt sure the old lady was referring to Fingers. "Not just the elephant," she said. "The whole caravan and trailer too."

"Aha!" said Ma Brackenbury. She stood herself a little straighter, stared into the horizon, and sucked on her long-stemmed clay pipe again. "That," she said, "presents more of a challenge."

Chapter Nine
Splash Down!

Getting Clip and Clop on board was easy enough if you knew the right people and, of course, Ma Brackenbury did. Remember that great big hulk of a fisherman by the name of Wellum? Of course you do. He simply crawled under Clip, stood up, and held on to her front legs with one hand and her back legs with the other – like a shepherd might hold a sheep – and climbed down the ladder on to the boat deck, which was now halfway down the harbour wall. Clip wasn't the slightest bit bothered –

or even that interested. Sunny had managed to find some of the juiciest thistles he'd seen all year, and Clip was merrily chewing away throughout the whole operation.

Clop was a little more concerned than his sister. As he was being carried to the edge of the wall, he brayed a few times but – despite the deafening "Hee-haw!" in his ear – Wellum gave a few soothing words of encouragement. (And Clop certainly enjoyed the rest of his thistles once he felt the solid wooden deck beneath his hooves.)

Getting Fingers aboard wasn't exactly straightforward either. He could potentially tip over the whole boat. With guidance and encouragement from Sunny, who (bravely) stayed sitting on top of him throughout, Fingers managed to step, gingerly, aboard. With the weight of a fully grown elephant pressing down on it, *The Merry Dance* leaned dangerously: tipping right down on one side and right up the other, causing a few wobbly, nervous moments. However, Sunny quickly got Fingers to the middle of the boat, levelling it out again, so it simply rocked on the surface. That done, he slipped off Fingers, who gave him a big hug with his trunk, lifting him right up off the deck and then back down with a bump.

That left the caravan itself.

Before Fingers had stepped aboard *The Merry Dance*, he'd pulled the caravan across a huge net laid out especially on the floor of the harbour wall. The rope making up the mesh was as thick as a man's arm. Now the four corners of the net were gathered together and – through a metal-lined loop – attached to the hook of a large crane.

Mr and Mrs Grunt stood and watched from the wall. Sunny, Mimi and the animals watched from the deck of the boat.

With the possible exception of Mr Grunt,

everyone was expecting the caravan that he and Old Mr Grunt had made to crack up under the strain: that, any minute now, it would fall to bits, and pieces of it would be raining down on them into the sea . . .

Ma Brackenbury gave the signal, and the crane came to life. When it slowly lifted the net, there were a few creaks and groans of protest from the structure, but the big CRACK never came. Next, the raised net was swivelled over the boat and – with Sunny making sure Fingers was well clear – it was slowly lowered on to the deck, where it was fixed in place.

Sunny clapped. Mimi let out a cheer. Fingers trumpeted (a happy trumpet, this time), the POGI said, "POGI!", and Mrs Grunt . . .

Mrs Grunt fell into the sea.

F-e-l-l i-n-t-o t-h-e s-e-a.

They hooked her out with the crane, water pouring from her pockets.

"You pushed me, mister!" she shouted in mid-air.

"Didn't touch you!" shouted Mr Grunt.

"Did!" Mrs Grunt insisted.

"Wish I had!" shouted Mr Grunt.

"And you did!" shouted Mrs Grunt.

"Hogwash!"

"Pigswill!"

"Inkwell!"

"Bottlebrush!"

And with that final insult, Mrs Grunt was lowered on to the harbour wall with a "squelch" as her waterlogged shoes touched the stonework.

"You're alive!" cried Mr Grunt, and threw his arms around his sodden wife as though he'd actually feared for her safety.

All that was left to be done was for Mr Grunt to have a quiet word with Ma Brackenbury (during which he handed her a wad of notes from the "expenses" envelope given to him by the man in the shadows in the tent in the field), and for them to wait for the captain, a certain Captain Haunch.

You see, it turned out that Mr Grunt hadn't only hired *The Merry Dance* but also someone to captain her, and Ma Brackenbury had chosen Haunch as the best man for the job.

While they were waiting, Sunny led Clip and Clop down a narrow ramp into the hold below. The donkeys seemed perfectly happy with this unusual arrangement, munching on their thistles and looking around their new, darker, surroundings with mild donkey interest. He and Mimi soon had an area of the wooden floor scattered with straw from their trailer, and they poured some oats into one bucket and some water into another.

"Not too full," said Mimi, "in case the boat lists."

"Lists?" asked Sunny.

"Tilts," said Mimi. "Rolls about in the sea."

Next, Sunny took the opportunity to explore the boat. He started off in the wheelhouse at the front of the deck, which housed the big wheel used to steer *The Merry Dance*, along with various other gizmos and dials. Next, he took a whirlwind tour around the cabins below.

Sunny had secretly hoped that there might be hammocks to sleep in, but there turned out to be little beds built into the side of the walls, to stop them sliding around when the vessel rolled about on the waves, he supposed.

What was *really* exciting was the porthole in the cabin he'd chosen as his own. The portholes in the outer cabins were small and round and made of (fairly) shiny brass. To open them, you had to unscrew a locking latch at the side. Once closed, they were watertight if rain and waves splattered against them. Why a small, round, brass window – with really

thick glass – should have seemed so exciting, I've no idea. But it was to Sunny.

There were more than enough cabins for all of them. There was also enough space for Fingers as well as Clip and Clop in the hold, if they'd been able to get him down there. There was no way the elephant could have fitted through the doorway and on the ramp the donkeys had used. The only opening big enough was a large hatchway but – without using the crane again – there was no way for Fingers to use it. He'd have to spend the voyage on deck (in the middle most of the time, if possible, so as not to rock the boat).

"He must stay put, see?" Ma Brackenbury had insisted. "If he don't, I won't be responsible for your safety and you'll owe me a new vessel. If you's don't drown first. Keep him in the middle. Keep things *balanced*."

The engine room was a dark and dingy place in the very bowels of the ship, which seemed to have water on the floor and smelled of oily machines. Sunny didn't spend much time in there. He had soon explored the whole ship from bow to stern. Or stern to bow. Or both.

Back on deck a while later, he was chatting to Fingers and feeding him a stale currant bun, when Mollusc appeared along the harbour wall in his turned-down wellies, with a very nattily dressed man a few paces behind him. Mollusc had a brief conversation with Ma Brackenbury, who then came over to the boat, scrimshaw-topped stick in hand.

She called out Mr Grunt's name, wisps of her unnaturally yellow hair blowing in the slight breeze.

He appeared from behind the wheelhouse.

"Huh?" said Mr Grunt.

"Sad to report that Cap'n Haunch has had a bit of a nasty fall, but I's found you an excellent replacement!" she said.

"It were me what found him," muttered Mollusc.

Mr Grunt looked over to the man next to Mollusc. He was wearing blue canvas shoes, a blue blazer with a gold anchor on the breast pocket, a white shirt open at the collar, and a blue cravat around his neck. On his head he wore a white cap with a blue peak (and embroidered gold anchor). He looked every inch a captain.

"You any good?" Mr Grunt called from the boat.

"I've sunk two vessels and beached another," said the captain, "which means I've experienced catastrophes and learned how to avoid them. I'm the best!"

His voice sounded very familiar to Sunny, who peered up at him, trying to make out his face from that distance.

Suddenly, Frizzle and Twist upped and flew away.

"Mr Lasenby!" Sunny gasped. And – surprise, surprise – he was right.

"Frizzle? Twist?" Mimi called up into the clear blue sky.

Rodders Lasenby began climbing down the iron-runged ladder set in the stone wall.

"Hello again," he said to Sunny and Mimi. "There's been an explosion at the Lasenby Destructions factory I was supposed to be visiting, so my meetings have been cancelled.

Couldn't have turned out better for you, huh? Onwards, I say. Onwards!"

He jumped from the last rung and gave a little skip as he landed on the deck.

"Amazing," said Sunny.

"Quite a remarkable coincidence," said Mimi, in such a way that made it clear that she was a girl who didn't *believe* in quite remarkable coincidences.

"Right time, right place," said Rodders Lasenby. "My luggage will be along in a moment."

Sunny heaved an inner sigh of relief, glad that someone else was having to carry it this time. "So you're a ship's captain?" he asked.

"In my spare time," Rodders Lasenby said. "Happy to help out." He looked around the deck of *The Merry Dance*. "What an ancient tub!" he exclaimed. "Love her!"

Mimi jabbed Sunny in the ribs with her elbow and jerked her head in a "come-and-have-a-private-chat-with-me-over-here" kind of way. So he went to have a private chat with her over there.

"What's his game?" whispered Mimi.

"What do you mean?" whispered Sunny.

"He *happens* to break down in front of the caravan on the way here. He *happens* to be happy to come all the way to Isaac's Port with us. That other captain, Lunch—"

"Haunch. Captain Haunch," Sunny corrected her.

"That other captain, Haunch, *happens* to have a mysterious accident –" Mimi made the word "accident" sound as if she meant anything *but* an accident. "– and Lasenby *happens* to be able to sail a boat . . ."

"*The Merry Dance* doesn't have sails,"

Sunny pointed out.

Mimi scowled. "You know what I mean."

"Yes," said Sunny. "Sorry."

"And," said Mimi, "*and* he happens to have the time to help out too!"

"I think you don't like Rodders Lasenby because Fizzle and Twist don't like him," said Sunny.

"Come on, Sunny!" said Mimi. "You can't tell me that you don't think the whole thing is a little bit odd? We're on some kind of a mission, in case you've forgotten? A mission involving a Person of Great Importance . . . A POGI who someone else –" she paused and looked over at Rodders Lasenby. "– may well want to get his hands on. I trust him even less than I trust Max and Martha. And that's saying something."

Chapter Ten
Dropping By

It was Mrs Grunt who gave Sunny the name Sunny. Perhaps she meant "Sonny" with an "o" (as in you-are-now-my-SON) but it was Mr Grunt who was the first one to write it down. And he wrote the name with a "u", and it stuck. The reason? Probably because Mrs Grunt has never seemed so happy as when he'd put that big-eared baby in her hairy, caring arms. Sunny had brought sunshine to their lives.

Up until then, Mrs Grunt's tattoos had all

seemed to be of rather gloomy subjects. There was the one which read "MUM" (and Mrs Grunt's mum was just about as gloomy as you can imagine, as you'll find out if you read *The Grunts in a Jam*). There was the tattoo of the human skull with a headache, and there was the one of the run-over hedgehog. The last one isn't quite as gloomy as it appears – even though there were tyre marks and everything – because she didn't have it done to remind her of a depressing accident, but as a way of remembering a really nice meal. (It might be a bit like you having a tattoo of a pizza slice. If you like pizza.) But, within weeks of Sunny becoming one of the family, she had a big tattoo of a sunflower done on her arm. (It's not a very good tattoo, by the way. But it's the thought that counts.)

If you're the sort of person who gets teary-eyed if you see a baby bunny with a limp, then you're probably thinking, "Ahhh, isn't that lovely!" If, however, you're one of those people who's so tough that you don't even wear a vest in REALLY cold weather, you're probably thinking, "Yerch!" (and counting the icicles under your armpits). Either way, remember that I'm just telling it how it was.

The first time Mr Grunt wrote down the name "SUNNY" it was in capital letters on the inside of a sweet wrapper. The wrapper was slightly greasy, so Mr Grunt had to go over some of the letters more than once (which always looks a bit messy). He was also resting the wrapper on his knee, rather than on a hard, flat surface (which didn't help matters either). If that wasn't bad enough, he was in the back of a moving caravan

181

(their only home at the time), on a stretch of particularly lumpy-bumpy country lane which Clip and Clop, their donkeys, had decided to explore. So, as you'll have gathered, the very first time Sunny's name was committed to paper, the end result was almost as weird and wonky as he looked in real life, what with his uneven ears and not forgetting – and who could forget? – those blue dresses he wore. Once Mr Grunt had written Sunny's name, he neatly folded the sweet wrapper and put it in the pocket of his only shirt with a pocket. The pocket nearest to his heart.

Now, I know that stealing other people's children is wrong. I nearly always sign a "Stealing Children is Wrong" petition if I'm asked to, and have even been on a Stealing Children Just Ain't Right march in Dublin – though, admittedly, I thought it was a queue for free cakes – but I don't want you to think that the Grunts were ALL BAD.

OK, so as you've seen, Mr Grunt had a pretty bad temper. He once punched the face of a floral clock for looking at him in a strange way, which is in itself a bit strange when you realise that a floral clock is simply a clock with a face made (mainly) of flowers. But when it came to being angry at people, about the worst thing he did was SHOUT. (Though shouting can be not-very-nice-either sometimes.) And, oh yes, wave his arms around a lot. And throw things. And kick things – electricity pylons, fibreglass tomatoes, melons, thin air – but not (usually) people.

Mr Grunt was shouting now. He was shouting so loudly that his mouth couldn't open any wider. It looked as if someone could pop a tennis ball inside it without it touching the sides. And his face. What about his face? I'll tell you about his face. It was really, really red again.

There were many things that Mrs Grunt loved about her husband – hard to imagine, I know, but it's true – and one such thing was that when he got really, really angry, he often went her favourite shade of red.

Mr Grunt was furious. He wanted to know who had been STUPID enough to put a great big box of chocolates on the bed next to him. He'd rolled over on to the box in his sleep and – because the box had the lid off – the chocolates had melted against his cheek. So when he got up he looked like someone who'd been pelted with mud . . . but he did smell rather nicer than usual.

"What idiot put chocolate in my bed?" he shouted, stumbling to his feet, only just avoiding stepping on Sharpie the stuffed hedgehog (which was excellent news for both of them). As he stomped barefoot across the room, he pulled some of the chocolates off his face and popped them in his mouth.

Mmmmm. They didn't taste bad. In fact, they tasted very good. His taste buds and brain were sending and receiving signals of general niceness and contentment. The result? Although he was still angry, and wanted to find out what BUFFOON had gone and stuffed chocolates in the bed, he was also experiencing a warm, positive, chocolatey glow.

Being creatures of habit, Mr and Mrs Grunt

had slept in the caravan on the deck of *The Merry Dance* that night – their first night after an uneventful first day at sea – even though they had the pick of the cabins. So it was on the caravan landing that Mr Grunt now met Mrs Grunt. This was the landing that usually doubled up as Sunny's bedroom, but *he'd* chosen a cabin – with a little brass porthole – to sleep in.

"Why have you gone and smeared yourself with the chocolates?" demanded Mrs Grunt, which was a reasonable question under the circumstances.

Mr Grunt spluttered like an ill-fitting lid on a kettle about to boil. He opened his mouth – showing two impressive rows of chocolate-coloured teeth – but no words came out. He didn't know which ones to use. He didn't know what to say.

At that moment, Sunny came bounding across the deck in his dress, his non-matching shoes clattering on the wood. He arrived just in time to see Mr Grunt peel a coffee creme off his forehead and pop it in his mouth.

"Happy birthday, Dad," he said, a smile spreading across his face. "I'm pleased you like the chocolates." (Though he did wonder why Mr Grunt had covered himself in them.)

Mr Grunt frowned. "Birthday?" he said.

Mrs Grunt nodded. "Birthday," she said.

Mr Grunt looked at the smiling boy. "You put these chocolates in my bed for my birthday?"

"*By* your bed," Sunny corrected him. "I wanted it to be a surprise when you woke up, so I put the box on your bedside table."

"And I took the lid off them later and put them on the bed next to you once I'd got up to cook you your surprise birthday breakfast

. . . " said Mrs Grunt. "So you wouldn't miss them."

"*Wouldn't miss them?*" said Mr Grunt. "I couldn't miss them, wife! I rolled all over them. It was a direct hit!" He paused. "And I didn't know anything about a surprise breakfast."

"That's because it's a surprise!" said Sunny. "Come on down, Dad." He turned and hurried back down the rickety stairs.

Mr Grunt followed him. "Thank you for the chocolates, Sunny," he grunted (quietly). "They're not bad." Mr Grunt could hardly hide his delight at the sight that greeted him on deck as he stepped out of the caravan into another bright, sunny morning. The others had obviously gone to a great deal of trouble to make him a truly splendid birthday breakfast.

Everything had been laid out on a table on deck. Mrs Grunt, Sunny and Mimi had brought this out of the caravan along with four kitchen chairs and their tin bath, which they'd upended and sat their wind-up gramophone on top. (A very old, very scratchy record was playing a dreary song about a missing pigeon.)

There was freshly squeezed juice, made from windfall apples that Sunny and Mimi had stuffed into an old pair of Mrs Grunt's tights, then beaten with an old meat-tenderising hammer, letting the juice out and keeping the pulp in. There was a sort of muesli-style cereal, though the little black squidgy bits might not

have been raisins but mouse droppings, and there was a fantastic roadkill fry-up which included everything from shredded car tyre "in crispy bacon strips" and generous portions of magpie, to part of a mud flap from a Land Rover (cut into mouth-watering shapes), and some nice pieces of squirrel meat, plus plenty of scrambled eggs and a tomato. All of this had been packed away and hidden from Mr Grunt until now, for his birthday surprise.

Mr Grunt was very moved by all the trouble Sunny, Mimi and even Mrs Grunt had gone to for his birthday, and he gave a big sniff before wiping his nose on the sleeve of his pyjama jacket. (The one the note that had started the whole adventure had been safety-pinned to.)

"This looks all right, this does," he grunted. He pulled out a chair at the end of the table and sat down. "We may as well eat then!"

And that's exactly what he was about to do when he felt something nudging at his elbow. He looked down to see the POGI holding out his string bag which had something wrapped up inside it.

"POGI," said the POGI (which should come as no surprise).

"A present?" asked Mr Grunt, taking the bag. "For me?"

The POGI nodded, his barrel tilting back and forth.

Mr Grunt pulled out the parcel. It was a large, round cheese wrapped in a Save-U-Lots paper bag. He gave it a good sniff.

"Thank you," said Mr Grunt. "Thank you very much." He sounded like he really meant it, and was that a tear in the corner of his eye? He reached for a plate of squirrel, and the birthday breakfast began.

Clip and Clop – who had been brought up on deck and put back in their trailer – were busy enjoying the last of their thistles. The donkeys barely looked up from their own meal as the others ate. All they could hear were knives and forks clattering against plates and contented chewing and slurping, along with the gentle hum of the boat's engine and the slapping of the water against the sides.

Hang on. That *was* the hum of the engine, wasn't it? Or was it the hum of bees?

BEES?

No, it wasn't bees.

Not bees.

No.

Phew.

It was an aeroplane – a bright-yellow twin-seater biplane – that was hurtling straight towards *The Merry Dance*! Well, not *straight* towards them exactly; it was spiralling like a corkscrew with its engine spluttering, but it was coming right at them.

The Grunts scattered. Mrs Grunt threw herself from her chair on to the deck. Sunny frantically tried to push his chair from the table but the legs were stuck in a groove between the planks, so he found the chair – and himself

– tilting backwards into the middle of a huge coil of rope. Mimi simply tried to make herself as flat and least crash-into-able as she could, narrowly avoiding an elephant "pancake" in the process. Fingers – the elephant himself – simply watched proceedings with interest.

Mr Grunt, meanwhile, had managed to crawl under the upturned tin bath on which Sunny had put the wind-up gramophone. It made an excellent hideaway, though only an idiot would think it would protect them from a crashing plane . . . which is why Mrs Grunt was also doing her best to get under it.

"Let me in, mister!" she shouted, trying to lift the bath.

"Keep away, wife!" Mr Grunt replied, with an echoing tinny voice from within. He was pulling the bath down around him as best he could.

"Aren't you supposed to protect me?" demanded Mrs Grunt.

"It's my birthday," said Mr Grunt. "My special day. I demand special treatment!"

"I'll give you special treatment, all right!" said Mrs Grunt.

She grabbed a huge wooden spoon from a bowl of squashed pigeon and treacle, and began beating the side of the old tin bath with it, to the rhythm of "Happy Birthday" which she started to sing loudly and terribly. From the outside, the old tin bath made quite a clanking sound. Inside the bath, it must have been like sitting inside a large bell when it was being struck by the clapper.

Mr Grunt whimpered and threw off the bath. Before you could say, "Victory!", Mrs Grunt had snatched it up and was busily climbing under it; pulling in her head last of all, like a tortoise retreating into its shell.

No sooner was she not-so-safely underneath than the plane spluttered over the boat, skimming the top of the wheelhouse (where a surprised Rodders Lasenby, in full captain's uniform, was gawping out of a side window) and – with a final death-rattle cough from the failing engine – plummeted into the sea.

Chapter Eleven

Rescue?

Whatever Rodders Lasenby was or wasn't up to, there's no denying that he knew how to steer a boat (as well as look good in a captain's cap). In next to no time he had *The Merry Dance* alongside the bright-yellow biplane, which at this stage was still above the water. Some planes are designed to land on the sea (which is why such planes are called "seaplanes", I suspect), but this wasn't one of them.

Although its engine was now silent, there

were strange creaking and graunching noises coming from the plane – a bit like a very large rumbling tummy – which didn't sound healthy. The right wing was snapped in the middle, with half of it pointing skyward, making it look like a weird yellow bird with a broken wing.

The pilot, who was in an open cockpit, calmly unfastened the seat belt criss-crossing their chest, and then – putting a hand on the yellow fuselage either side of the seat – heaved themselves out, swinging their legs on to the edge of the plane. Next, the pilot lifted the huge pair of chrome-framed flying goggles from their eyes.

Sunny, Mr and Mrs Grunt and Mimi were all crowded together in a little group, leaning over the portside of the boat. The POGI, who'd gone back below deck to eat some cheese of his own, came to find out what all the fuss was about. (Fingers, meanwhile, was sitting next to the open-topped trailer containing Clip and Clop, roughly in the centre of the boat.)

"It's Speedy McGinty!" cried Sunny.

"Speedy?" said Mr Grunt in amazement. "That's *Speedy*?"

"Ahoy there!" shouted Speedy McGinty. The biplane gave a sudden shudder and big bubbles erupted on to the surface of the sea.

"Man the lifeboats!" shouted Mr Grunt.

"Mash a pound of bananas!" shouted Mrs Grunt.

"Don't be so absurd!" said Mr Grunt.

"Don't be afraid of the dark!" said Mrs Grunt.

"Pull yourself together!" shouted Mr Grunt.

"Pull yourself apart!" shouted Mrs Grunt.

The pair were now running around the deck

like ants without a chief ant with a clipboard telling them what to do.

"Don't you fret," Speedy McGinty called across from the slowly sinking plane. "I ain't the world's best swimmer, but I can float."

Rodders Lasenby, with his captain's cap on his head, leaned around the open doorway of the wheelhouse.

"Sunny!" he called. "Come here, would you? There's a good chap." He pulled a few levers and the noise of the engine got louder but, instead of circling, *The Merry Dance* stayed pretty much in one place. The sea churned around them.

Sunny, meanwhile, dashed over to join him.

"Listen," said Rodders Lasenby, loud

enough only for the boy to hear. "We don't have much time and things could turn really bad, which is a good thing because I think better under pressure. It's not a matter of how good a swimmer that person is, or how well they float. If the plane goes down, it could suck her down with it." He rubbed his beautifully shaved chin, releasing wafts of expensive aftershave. "I need you to get Fingers over to the side and see if you can get him to reach her with his trunk. But slowly does it . . ."

"I'll try," said Sunny. "He usually does what I ask, especially if I encourage him with buns!"

Very slowly, Sunny started to lead Fingers over to the side of the boat and it tilted under his weight. "Everybody over to the other side!" Sunny shouted, and even Mr and Mrs Grunt did as they were told, though they were soon sliding back towards the elephant.

Of course, Fingers had walked around the deck of *The Merry Dance* a little since stepping aboard, but certainly not right over to the eeeeeeeeeeeeeeeedge.

Sunny remembered Ma Brackenbury's warning about not letting the elephant rock the boat.

The Merry Dance tilted further still. The bottom half of the caravan's stable door opened and three or four melons bounced down the back steps and on to the deck. They rolled around like green balls in a giant pinball machine. Mimi dashed up the tilting deck to close the door, just as a wet cake of soap shot out like an escaped lemon-scented rodent making a bid for freedom. She slammed the stable door shut. Top and bottom.

The caravan itself, of course, was firmly chained to the deck.

The tin bath, meanwhile, slid across the slanting deck until it bumped up against a huge coil of rope with an impressive clank. The breakfast table stuttered a few metres before hitting the rim of the hatch down to the hold, causing much of the food – if you can call it that – and some of the plates – if you can call *them* that: they were upturned hubcaps – to fall. Chairs toppled, and the wind-up gramophone hit Mrs Grunt's ankles, causing her to yelp.

The POGI lost his footing and fell to the deck, rolling in his barrel on his side towards the Fingers side of the boat, reaching an impressive speed before smashing into the back of Mr Grunt's legs, causing him to fall backwards with a muffled "ARG!"

Mrs Grunt laughed.

Twice.

Then once again, for the fun of it.

In position now, Sunny started throwing currant buns into the sea in front of him. A puzzled Fingers stretched out his trunk to try to reach them. "Jump in, Speedy!" Sunny shouted. "And grab a bun!"

Speedy McGinty didn't need asking twice. She slid off the side of the bright-yellow biplane into the sea with a brief splash, and grabbed the nearest soggy bun floating on the surface and waved it above her head.

"Look, buns, Fingers," said Sunny. "Buns!"

As soon as the bun-clutching Speedy was less than a trunk's length from the boat, Fingers wrapped his trunk around her – in the way he hugged Sunny – and lifted her up out of the sea, over the side and on to *The Merry Dance*.

Safely on board, Speedy McGinty sat on the deck in a pool of seawater. "Nicely done!" she said, and handed Fingers the soggy bun, which he gratefully received.

A moment later there was a sound like a giant sucking on a huge boiled sweet, and the bright-yellow biplane began to disappear beneath the surface of the sea. And was gone. Where moments before there'd been this wounded yellow feat of engineering, now there was only the rippling surface of greenish-blue water.

The Merry Dance wobbled in its wake.

Everyone looked on in silence. A moment later there was what can only be described as a sea-like "burp" and something erupted to the surface. It was Speedy McGinty's folded lightweight wheelchair! Mr Grunt grabbed it with a boat hook and flipped it on board.

"My wheels!" said Speedy. She couldn't have looked happier.

After everything had been picked up from all around the deck, Mr Grunt's birthday breakfast turned into a birthday brunch, with an extra place laid for Speedy McGinty. She didn't seem to have much of an appetite, though (which was hardly surprising with the "food" on offer).

"I came to warn you," she said.

"About what?" asked Mrs Grunt. "Low-flying planes?"

Mr Grunt grunted at that.

"About the people who paid me a visit not long after you did," she said. She went on to tell them that, not long after Sunny came to borrow the maps and charts, another unexpected visitor turned up on her doorstep. He was a thin, hairy, jet-black-moustached chap calling himself Max. (There is actually

208

the word "moustachioed" to describe someone having a moustache, but I find it far too silly-looking and refuse to use it.)

At first, Max pretended to be lost and claimed he'd knocked to ask directions. But when he recognised Speedy as the (really quite) famous Speedy McGinty, the man (and his moustache) seemed to get all excited and even asked for an autograph. Speedy thought that there was something not-quite-right about the way he was behaving, and when he commented on the elephant footprints in the earth, she became even more suspicious.

Then she heard the yapping. Something – or someone – was bothering Petal. It soon became obvious who: a lank-haired woman came charging down the trophy-lined hallway and out through the open front door . . . with a small dog clamped to her bottom.

"Get this thing off me!" she yelled, but Max was too busy turning-and-running to help her. It was only when they'd both run out of the garden and part way up the lane that Petal let go and scuttled back to her mistress, a torn piece of shorts between her canine canines.

"But I thought you said Petal didn't bite?" said Sunny.

"Only intruders!" said Speedy, with a flush of pride. "Petal makes a great little guard dog. At first I thought that good-for-nothin' pair were thieves after my trophies or some story to sell to the newspapers. Then I realised that the only thing that was missing was the piece of paper you left on the piano, Sunny, with the list of the place names you needed maps and charts for."

"They're the couple calling themselves Max and Martha," said Sunny. "No doubt about it.

We met them outside The Happy Pig and we saw them snooping around in Isaac's Port too, trying to get a room in O'Neill's Hotel."

"They *must* be out to get the POGI or to stop him reaching his destination!" said Mimi.

"That's what I reckoned," said Speedy McGinty. She looked at the POGI. "I assume that's you?" she said.

"POGI," said the POGI.

"So I went to the airfield and fired up *The Canary*."

"You set fire to a canary?" gawped Mrs Grunt.

"Don't be a fool, wife!" said Mr Grunt. "'Fired up' means 'got excited' . . . She excited a canary!"

"*The Canary* is my plane . . . *was* my plane," said Speedy McGinty, with a sigh. "And I mean I got the engine going."

"Do you think it was sabotage?" asked Mimi. "Do you think someone deliberately messed with the plane to stop you reaching us? You could have been killed."

"You could have hit *us*," muttered Mrs Grunt. She gave Sharpie, who was on her lap, a hug. Because he was a stuffed hedgehog, this wasn't a great idea. "OUCH!" she said. "*Bad* hedgehog!" and slapped him. "OUCH!" she said again, sucking her sore hand.

"Sabotage? No, dear," said Speedy. "There ain't no way anyone would know I was goin' to use the plane, and they wouldn't have had time to do anything to it, anyhow."

"Then what do you think happened?"

"My mechanic, Earl, is what happened . . . or *didn't* happen. He swore blind that he'd fix a problem with the fuel pump and I thought he had . . . but he can't have done."

"And here you are," said Mr Grunt. He leaned across the table and took Speedy McGinty's hand in his own. "You lost your parrot—"

"Canary," Mimi corrected him.

Mr Grunt scowled. "Your plane . . . and could have lost your life trying to warn us. I don't know what to say, Speedy."

"That's what's puzzling me," Sunny whispered to Mimi. "Once Dad even tried to steal her door knocker, so why did she go to so much trouble to warn him? It's not as if they're best friends or anything. He won't even go in the house. He just shouts through the window!"

When the others were deep in conversation again, Mimi turned back to Sunny. "I've just thought of something else," she whispered.

"What?" Sunny whispered back.

"Lasenby's uniform," whispered Mimi.

"What about it?"

"If Rodders Lasenby had no idea he was going to be captaining a boat, how come he had his whole captain's uniform with him?"

Sunny swallowed a piece of acorn-and-wood-shavings pie. He didn't have an answer to that.

Chapter Twelve

"Land Ahoy!"

Mimi and Sunny sat next to each other on the bed in his cabin.

"Do you think we're in danger?" asked Mimi.

"Living in a falling-down manor house with missing floorboards is dangerous," said Sunny. "Scraping squashed animals off busy roads for food, that's dangerous too . . . but, as for this?" He shrugged. "Who knows?"

"I wonder if the man who gave your dad the job in the first place is a good guy or a bad guy?" said Mimi. She'd put on a fresh splash of her homemade (pink) rose-petal perfume so was smelling perfectly pinkish.

"I hadn't thought of that," Sunny admitted. "Because we're good guys I kind of assumed we were *working* for the good guys."

Mimi looked at him through her pink-tinted spectacles.

"But would you call – er – Mr Grunt one of the good guys, Sunny? He did steal you off a washing line, remember . . ."

"But a baby shouldn't be hanging by the ears from a washing line in the first place," said Sunny, "so in a way you could say that he . . . that he rescued me." His expression changed.

"What is it?" asked Mimi.

"It's just that I've never thought of it that way before . . . At least, not been able to put it into words. He *rescued* me . . ."

Mimi didn't seemed convinced, but was sensitive enough to change the subject.

"And another thing," she said.

"What?" asked Sunny.

"For all we know, the POGI himself is a villain!"

"That's true." Sunny nodded. "And I don't get where Speedy McGinty fits into all of this."

Mimi stood up. "Do you know what we've got?"

"No, what?"

"A load of questions and no answers," said Mimi.

That night – their second at sea – there was a storm. It wasn't serious as storms go, but Mr Grunt was left feeling very green around the

gills. This is another way of saying seasick, which is another way of saying that he spent most of his time either: (a) feeling sick; (b) being sick; or (c) feeling sick while being sick.

The first time he was sick, he wasn't ready for it so was sick into the nearest thing: an upturned tortoise shell that the Grunts used as a bowl for keeping non-matching socks in (until there were enough of them in there for Sunny to start matching them up as pairs again).

Mrs Grunt was OUTRAGED. "What did you go and do that for, you swing-bin?" she demanded.

"Take a wild guess," whimpered Mr Grunt.

"To get me REALLY angry?" said Mrs Grunt.

Mr Grunt had his hand in front of his face. "Don't be so stupid, wife!" he said, trying to make sure that it was only *words* that came out of his mouth.

"To spoil our Sock Night?" said Mrs Grunt. (Not that they actually had a Sock Night to spoil.)

"BECAUSE I'M FEELING SICK!" Mr Grunt blurted, as he stood up and charged out of the room, out of the caravan, across the rain-swept, rolling deck – stepping in a pile of

 elephant poo along the way – over to the side, where he threw up.

(I'm sorry, but there it is.)

And there he stayed. All the other times he was sick, it was out of everyone's way. Unless the wind changed.

After a while, he felt someone slip their small hand into his. "Sunny?" groaned Mr Grunt, happy for the concern and the company. He looked around. It wasn't Sunny.

"POGI!" said the POGI, squeezing his hand.

"POGI!" said Mr Grunt, squeezing his hand back. He felt strangely comforted by the barrel-wearing man. Then he stuck his rain-stained head back over the side and was sick again. He was beginning to regret the rat sandwich he'd had with his bedtime glass of fox's milk.

Morning came and with it calm seas and a sight of land.

"Land ahoy!" shouted an excited Mimi, pointing at the sandy coastline.

"Yee-haa!" said Speedy McGinty, like cowboys do when they're rounding up cattle. She spun her wheelchair in a complete circle.

Rodders Lasenby leaned out of the door of

the wheelhouse and did a thumbs-up with one thumb, so why it isn't called a "thumb-up", I have no idea.

Sunny was busy cooking breakfast for everyone except the POGI, who, once again, seemed to be eating his way through what remained of his cheeses, in the privacy of his own cabin. On hearing Mimi's cry, Sunny dashed out of the caravan kitchen for a quick look at where they were heading, then dashed back in again.

Mr Grunt appeared in the kitchen, looking an unusual shade of grey.

"You look dreadful, Dad," said Sunny, tending a pan of frying toadstools.

"You should have seen me last night, Sunny," muttered Mr Grunt.

"Are you handing over the POGI to Mrs Bayliss today?" Sunny asked.

"Maybe today. Maybe tomorrow," said Mr Grunt. "I'll be glad when this whole messy business is over."

Sunny pushed the toadstools around the pan with a wooden spatula. "Why did you agree to do this in the first place, Dad?" he asked.

Mr Grunt plonked himself at the kitchen table. He didn't smell too good. "Excitement," said Mr Grunt. "Adventure. The chance to annoy your mother in new surroundings."

"Are you being paid?"

"Kind of."

Sunny wasn't sure he liked the sound of "kind of". The last time Mr Grunt had been given a big payment it turned out to be Fingers.

That part hadn't bothered Sunny. He'd been delighted, in fact. Especially because Fingers had ended up belonging to him (and him to Fingers) . . . but his dad had done some dirty double-crossing along the way.

"Can you keep a secret, Sunny?" asked the rather seasick Mr Grunt.

"Of course I can, Dad."

"You mustn't tell your mother."

"Promise."

"I'm going to miss that little POGI. I'm used to having him around."

"He's certainly no trouble," Sunny admitted. A thought suddenly occurred to him. "You *are* going to complete this job you've been given, aren't you, Dad? You're going to stick to your instructions and deliver him to this Mrs Bayliss lady, whoever she is?"

The toadstools were evenly browned on all

sides now, and Sunny served them up on to plates with the spatula.

"Yes, I'm going to hand the POGI over," said Mr Grunt. "But I'll still miss him." He got back to his feet. The smell of the fried food was making his stomach churn all over again.

After breakfast had been eaten, the plates and cutlery washed up and put away, Fingers, Clip and Clop fed and watered, and elephant dung shovelled up and tipped overboard, preparations were made to land.

It was then that Rodders Lasenby made his surprise announcement. "There's no harbour on the island," he said. "I checked the sea charts and the water isn't deep enough for us to take *The Merry Dance* right ashore."

"Are you sure about that?" said a puzzled Speedy McGinty from her gleaming

wheelchair.

"Most definitely, dear lady," said the captain. "If we tried to get too close, we'd hole the hull and could all drown . . . which is good. It means we get to use that rather nice rowing boat instead. Splendid!" He cut the engine and dropped anchor. The sea was calm, and they could barely feel *The Merry Dance* rocking on the surface beneath their feet.

"Well, I'm going to double-check them charts!" announced Speedy, speeding off across the deck in the opposite direction.

"As you wish," said Rodders Lasenby, but

he looked far from pleased.

"We can't fit Fingers, the donkeys and the caravan in a rowing boat, you jumped-up fancy teacake!" said Mrs Grunt with her usual charm.

"Which is why they'll have to stay on board," said Rodders Lasenby, straightening his natty cravat.

"Then why did we bring them along in the first place?" demanded Mrs Grunt.

"To confuse the enemy?" suggested Sunny. "That's right, isn't it, Dad? You're covering our tracks?"

Mr Grunt, who was beginning to look a little more human or, at least, a little more like his almost-human-looking self, was about to reply, but Mrs Grunt got in first.

"I'll tell you why we didn't just leave them at Isaac's Port," she said. "Because Mr Grunt

is an *idiot*, that's why."

"Takes one to know one, dumbbell!"

"Carpet beater!" said Mrs Grunt.

"Foliage!" said Mr Grunt.

"Foliage?!?" said Mrs Grunt, quivering with rage.

Sunny left them arguing, and went to prepare the rowing boat with Mimi under the instruction of Captain Lasenby, while Speedy McGinty searched through her beloved map and charts. The only one she *couldn't* find seemed to be the one of the island and surrounding sea. "Now, where did it get to?" she muttered.

The rowing boat was lowered over the side by means of ropes and a pulley and the first to climb the rope ladder down the outside of *The Merry Dance* and into the rowing boat, bobbing alongside, was Mr Grunt, followed

by the POGI (because he had to be there), then Mrs Grunt (because she insisted on going too). Rodders Lasenby had suggested that Sunny also go "because," as he'd whispered to the boy, "you're obviously the sensible one." It was already a tight squeeze, but Mimi hadn't come this far to stay behind, so she managed to find a space. Even to Sunny's inexperienced eyes, the rowing boat looked very low in the water.

Peering at them over the side of *The Merry Dance*, Captain Lasenby looked concerned. "Your combined weight is too heavy. One of you is going to have to come back on board."

"Not me," said Mr Grunt, crossing his arms defiantly. "This is MY important top-secret mission."

"Nor me," said Mrs Grunt. "Where idiot-chops goes, I go." She gave her man a loving slap on the back.

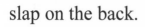

"POGI!" said the POGI.

"You *have* to stay," Sunny reminded him.

"I'll come back aboard," said Mimi. She'd loved to have gone, but realised that if anyone was surplus baggage, she was.

"Of course, the POGI could always take his barrel off," said Rodders Lasenby. "That would free up some weight."

"No!" said Mr Grunt and Sunny together.

"And I for one don't want to see barrel-boy here in the naughty-naked-nude," said Mrs Grunt, with the most indignant of indignant snorts.

Mimi was already standing up again, causing the little rowing boat to rock precariously.

"Whoaaa!" called Speedy McGinty. "Careful, honey!"

"No, wait," said Rodders Lasenby. "I've

had an idea. You sit back down, Mimi, and you come back up here for a moment, please, POGI."

And it was as simple as that. The POGI got to his feet and – supported by helping hands from the seated Grunts, Mimi and Sunny – stepped between them on the little bobbing rowing boat, and climbed the rope ladder up the outside of *The Merry Dance*.

Once he reached the top, Captain Lasenby put out a helping hand and heaved him aboard. Moments later there was a sudden unexplained THUD . . . and Rodders Lasenby was pulling in the ladder.

"Now, hold on there!" Speedy McGinty

called from across the deck. "What you playin' at?"

"Hey!" said Sunny, leaping to his feet in the boat. "What's happening?"

"SIT DOWN!" barked Mr Grunt.

Sunny sat down. The boat stopped rocking so violently.

"Sorry, chaps!" said Rodders Lasenby, peering back at them over the side. He raised his captain's cap politely. "Slight change of plan."

"Change of plan?" Mrs Grunt shouted back up in surprise.

"Change of plan." Lasenby nodded.

"What did you think he said, wife?" muttered Mr Grunt. "Change of tyre? Change of underwear?"

"Plan," Rodders Lasenby repeated, beginning to look a little annoyed at the interruptions. "I have some clients who are paying me handsomely to deliver this POGI to *them*."

"Good for you!" shouted Mrs Grunt, who had no idea what was going on.

"No!" shouted Mr Grunt in rage. "That's BAD!"

"*Bad* for you, then," shouted Mrs Grunt. "Like cheese before bedtime. That's bad for you." She went as if to stand up, but Sunny put a calming hand on her arm.

"I do feel rather sorry about this," said Rodders Lasenby, "but there's something so awfully *exciting* about being a double-crossing good-for-nothing!"

With a cry of "Not so fast!", Speedy McGinty reached him just as he was busy unfastening the ropes attaching the rowing boat to *The Merry Dance*. Job done, he turned and grabbed both arms of her wheelchair to stop her ramming into his knees with it, like a battering ram.

"It's nothing personal, you know!" he called out, gripping on to the chrome so tight his knuckles whitened. "You have oars. You can row to the island. It could be fun! Even good exercise! But by the time you raise the alarm I'll be long gone."

"You gargoyle!" shouted Mrs Grunt. "You fledgling! You tramp's pants!"

"You hand-towel! You pig's trotter! You OVEN GLOVE!" shouted Mr Grunt.

"Why are you doing this?" demanded Mimi from the boat.

"Spot of bother at Lasenby Destructions," Rodders Lasenby called down, still gripping the wheelchair and trying to ignore the blows Speedy McGinty was raining down on his tummy with her tightly balled fists. "Bit of a cash-flow problem. The cash keeps flowing *out* and I need bucket-loads of cash to flood *in*. And they're paying me handsomely for delivering the POGI to them."

"The POGI!?" Sunny shouted. He had forgotten about the POGI. "What have you done with him?!" He felt so helpless, the two boats already drifting apart.

"I just gave him a bonk on the head, but he'll be fine," said Rodders Lasenby with a sheepish grin. "The barrel took the brunt of the bashing."

"This is kidnapping!" said Mimi.

"This is madness!" said Speedy McGinty. "You'll never—"

"It's been lovely meeting you all," Rodders Lasenby interrupted. "And I really mean that. Such a pleasure. But I have a rendezvous to keep." He gave Speedy's wheelchair an almighty SHOVE and it went speeding back across the deck with Speedy in it. A minute or so later, the anchor was pulled up and the engine spluttered to life.

Mimi frowned at Sunny. "See," she said. "I told you we shouldn't trust him."

Rodders Lasenby turned *The Merry Dance* in a great arc across the surface of the sea and began heading back the way they'd come.

"And we'll never catch up with them now," Sunny sighed.

Chapter Thirteen
Surprise!

Technically speaking, Sunny and the others hadn't been cast adrift. They hadn't been left helpless, to go wherever the sea currents took them. As Rodders Lasenby had so rightly said, they had oars, so could row . . . in theory.

The problem was, of course, the Grunts.

If you find yourself in an emergency situation with a bunch of people on a boat, two of the *last* people you'd want to share that confined space with would be – drum roll – Mr and Mrs Grunt. (No surprises there, then.)

"Your fault," said Mrs Grunt.

"Yours," said Mr Grunt.

"I knew that captain was a bandicoot!" said Mrs Grunt.

"Didn't."

"Did."

"Liar!"

"Not."

"Bottletop!"

"Leaf-mould." With that, Mrs Grunt picked up the nearest thing and tried to throw it at Mr Grunt. It was one of the oars, and it fell into the water and went floating away on the surface of the sea.

"Toll booth!" shouted Mr Grunt, throwing himself overboard to swim after the escaping oar. Only, of course, he couldn't swim, and his sudden departure made the boat rock violently.

Mrs Grunt folded her arms and leaned over the side to watch Mr Grunt flail *his* arms around desperately and gulp down seawater as he gasped for breath.

Sunny and Mimi, meanwhile, leaned over the side and grabbed an arm each. After much heaving and almost as much ho-ing, they managed to get Mr Grunt half into the boat, and he managed the last half himself.

He sat on the plank seat, dripping into the bottom of the rowing boat. "HA!" he said.

"We need to head for shore," said Sunny, sensibly.

"How?" said Mr Grunt. "Old Bunny-Slippers here –" he jerked his head in the direction of Mrs Grunt "– has lost an oar."

"Didn't," Mrs Grunt insisted.

"Did."

"M—"

"We've still got *one*," Sunny interrupted.

"But we'll just end up going round in circles, Sunny," said Mr Grunt.

"Not if we can make another oar out of something," said Sunny.

"Great idea!" said Mimi. "How about the plank seat you're sitting on, Mrs Grunt? It's thinner than this one. More oar-like."

Mrs Grunt stood up to inspect it . . .

. . . and promptly fell overboard.

As Sunny and Mimi fished her out, Sunny

began to wonder whether his parents would simply end up taking it in turns to end up in the sea.

Back aboard *The Merry Dance*, Speedy McGinty was facing a rather different problem: Rodders Lasenby.

"You won't get away with this!" she said, once again wheeling her chair right up against his well-dressed knees.

"With the greatest respect," said the dirty double-crossing captain, and chairman of the failing Lasenby Destructions, "I can't see how one person in a gleaming wheelchair can hope to stop an experienced captain on a ship out at sea." He gripped the arms of her chair again. "And, I might add, I think you're extremely ungrateful considering I had you fished out of the sea." He pushed her back, but only half a metre or so this time.

"I was wondering 'bout that," confessed Speedy. "Why rescue me in the first place?"

"Madam, I'm not a murderer, just a good-for-nothing." He smiled his most gentlemanly smile.

"Big mistake, Lasenby," said Speedy McGinty. "Don't tell me you fell for the I-just-came-to-warn-you story I told Cankle." Now it was her turn to give a pearly-white grin.

"Cankle?" Rodders Lasenby raised an eyebrow.

"Mr Grunt," said Speedy McGinty, speedily correcting herself.

"Your crashing *The Canary* was real enough," said Rodders Lasenby.

"True," said Speedy McGinty, "but I ain't working alone." She thrust a hand inside her flying jacket and pulled out –

A walkie-talkie? A ship-to-shore telephone? A homing device? A gun? A telescopic truncheon? A beard of bees?

I just *know* you're dying to find out.

None of the above. Speedy McGinty pulled out –

– a stale currant bun.

Fingers – who'd been watching the whole proceedings, from Sunny and the others going over the side of the boat to the man in the funny uniform bashing the POGI in the upturned barrel over the head – sniffed the air. The fingers-like tip of his trunk quivered in anticipation. He smelled his favourite food: a slightly squashed, stale currant bun.

Sunny had told him to stay in the middle of the boat while he was gone. But the boy had *also* told him to listen to Ms McGinty, because she'd be looking after him while the captain was looking after the boat. And Ms McGinty was calling him over, and there was a stale bun involved: a *lovely* stale bun.

Fingers ambled over to Speedy and the bun. His elephant steps were elegant and careful, as an elephant's steps always are, but there was nothing he could do about his weight . . . and the boat listed to one side again.

Being a racing model, there were no brakes on Speedy McGinty's chair. To stop herself rolling, she had to hold on to the wheels, but only *after* she'd freed her hands by giving him his bun. He looked at her with those intelligent eyes of his as he munched slowly, making the most of the small treat.

"Get that animal back to the middle!" said Rodders Lasenby. "NOW!" He'd grabbed on to the doorway to the wheelhouse to keep himself steady.

"What makes you think that this prince among elephants will listen to one iddy-biddy person in a wheelchair?" she asked innocently.

Then she turned to Fingers. "He's a bad man," she told the elephant. "A real BAD man."

Clip and Clop looked at Rodders with their don't-mess-with-the-animals donkey-eyes. They gave Fingers a bray of support from their trailer. (With the flap closed and bolted at the back, they weren't in a position to offer a helping hoof.)

Before Rodders Lasenby could say, "What on bally earth is happening?", he found a trunk being wrapped around him like a hungry python squeezing its prey, and he was lifted high up into the air.

"Put me down!" he yelled. "Put me down!"

This wasn't the most original thing to say under the circumstances but it got the point across.

Fingers put him down all right. He dropped him through the open hatch into the hold.

"Oofff!" said Rodders Lasenby as his head hit a bale of straw, before he drifted off into an unnatural sleep. He dreamed of his mother giving him a good telling-off in front of all the Lasenby Destructions board members. He didn't like it one bit.

It didn't take long for Speedy McGinty to catch up with the rowing boat. She pulled herself out of her wheelchair into the captain's chair behind the wheel, so she had no problem seeing out of the wheelhouse windows.

The POGI, meanwhile, had fully recovered from his ill-treatment. He was standing on deck acting as lookout, proving once and for all that there MUST have been eye holes or a tiny slit in that barrel *somewhere*.

It wasn't that long before he caught sight of Sunny and the others, and alerted Speedy McGinty by letting out an excited "POGI!" and pointing.

Fingers trumpeted excitedly, causing Clip and Clop to bray.

Speedy McGinty, used to driving and piloting all types of craft, steered *The Merry Dance* alongside them with the ease of a consummate professional. (Consummate means "showing a high degree of skill", and shouldn't be confused with consommé, which

248

is a clear soup.)

In the rowing boat, they'd heard the boat's engine getting nearer and nearer and wondered why Rodders Lasenby had changed his plans. Then Mimi spotted the POGI up on deck.

"Look!" she cried. "It's the POGI!"

"POGI!" cried the POGI, leaping up and down excitedly. The others had only been in the rowing boat for about an hour but it seemed so much longer, perhaps because of the thought of what might have happened if Rodders Lasenby had succeeded.

"I don't understand," said Mrs Grunt. "What in the name of bent bottletops is happening?"

The POGI was busy unrolling the rope ladder.

"The POGI," said a triumphant Mr Grunt. "The POGI's taken control!" He thought he'd never see the little barrel-covered chap again and was absolutely delighted.

There was much back-slapping and congratulations for Speedy McGinty, the POGI and Fingers once everyone was back aboard *The Merry Dance* and their story had been told.

Mr Grunt had made it to the top of the rope ladder up the side of the boat before losing his footing and falling, grabbing Mrs Grunt as he fell, so I don't want you to think that "once they were back on board" was quite as simple a process as it may have first sounded. They had to be fished out again.

One at a time.

With the boat hook.

The pair of them looked soggier than an over-dunked ginger-nut biscuit (but didn't smell as nice).

For his part in the rescue, Fingers was awarded extra buns, and given a quiet word of extra praise by Sunny when they were alone together.

Speedy McGinty was sure to let everyone know what vocal support – that's "hee-haw"s of encouragement – Clip and Clop had given, while Mrs Grunt, meanwhile (still dripping wet), practised a whole selection of made-up-as-you-go-along knots as she tied up Rodders Lasenby in the hold.

"Apart from the dreadful things I do for money, I'm not a bad man," he insisted. "Then again, I'm not that *good* either."

"Put a sock in it!" said Mrs Grunt, stuffing precisely one of those in his mouth to shut him up. Fortunately for the captain, it wasn't one of the mismatched socks that had been in the tortoise shell the night before. But it wasn't particularly *clean* either.

Of course, Mr Grunt still had the POGI to deliver, but Speedy McGinty had made an interesting discovery when studying the missing – and slightly chewed – sea chart that she'd found hidden in Clip and Clop's trailer.

"Lasenby made the whole thing up about there being no deep-water harbour on the island," she said. "There's one right here at Hydrock Cove." She pointed at a place on the chart. "We can sail right in and drop anchor."

"Why did he lie about that too, I wonder?" muttered Mr Grunt. "The man is a . . . a . . ."

"Compost heap?" Mrs Grunt suggested helpfully, blinking in the daylight.

"Precisely, wife!" said Mr Grunt. "Exactly! Nothing more than a comp—" He stopped and glared at her. "Don't be so ridiculous!"

"Lasenby lied about there being no harbour to get us all into the rowing boat and out of the way!" said Sunny. "It was much easier for him to seize control with us all bobbing about down there."

"A compost heap, indeed," muttered

Mr Grunt.

"Well, he didn't bargain for Ms McGinty and Fingers!" Mimi beamed, and well she might, for, with Rodders Lasenby bound and gagged in his cabin, the two humming birds – Frizzle and Twist – had appeared out of clear blue skies and were now hovering around above her head once more.

So Speedy McGinty skilfully took *The Merry Dance* right into the natural harbour at Hydrock Cove, and the others went ashore, leaving her in charge of the prisoner.

Once ashore, the motley crew of Mr and Mrs Grunt, Sunny, Mimi – with Frizzle and Twist – and not forgetting the POGI, of course, strode up the beach, along the causeway and into town.

People gawped. Mr and Mrs Grunt looked unusual enough; Sunny with his wonky ears, sticky-up hair and blue dress was always worth a gawp; the extraordinarily pink Mimi with her halo of hummingbirds was an undeniable eye-catcher; but on that day it was the POGI who really stole the show. A walking barrel was a sight to see.

Mr Grunt consulted a (rather soggy) list of instructions. "We need to find a row of seven fishermen's cottages, with a garage in the middle called Stan's Motor Repairs.

We should find Mrs Bayliss in the cottage immediately to the right of it, as we face the front doors."

"What if I *refuse* to face the front doors, husband?" Mrs Grunt demanded. "What if I turn my back on them?"

"Then it'll simply be the house on your left," said Sunny.

"You mean it'll have moved?"

Sunny sighed. "Never mind."

It took them a while to find the row of cottages with Stan's Motor Repairs in the middle. It was on a cobbled street on a steep hillside.

"There it is!" said Mr Grunt, and he began to stride up the hill.

All being well, his mission would soon be at an end.

Chapter Fourteen
Unlucky For Some

Mr and Mrs Grunt and the others were standing outside Stan's Motor Repairs.

"Mrs Bayliss's cottage must be that one," said Mr Grunt. He pointed.

"I'll knock," said Mrs Grunt, striding up to the front door.

"No," said Mr Grunt, lovingly shoving her aside. "This is *my* adventure. I'll knock." He had just raised his fist and was about to pummel the wood with it, when a motorbike roared into view.

This was the first
vehicle any of them had seen on the island
and it was noisy. It was hard to see the driver
because he or she was dressed from head to
toe in bike leathers. Attached to the motorbike
was a sidecar, however, in which sat a very
familiar-looking figure. At least, his jet-black
moustache looked familiar. (When I say "his",
I mean that he'd got to wear it this time.)

"It's Max!" cried Mimi.

Before anyone knew what was happening,
Max had leaned out of the speeding sidecar,
snatched the barrel-wearing POGI and sped
off with him kicking and screaming sideways

on his lap.

They watched them go in a splutter of exhaust fumes.

One minute here. The next minute there . . .

. . . whizzing down the hill, little legs kicking helplessly in the air, like an upturned hermit crab.

"What do we do now?" said Sunny, feeling helpless. Mimi frantically looked around for inspiration.

Mr Grunt was busy shouting a stream of abuse, which didn't help the POGI but it made *him* feel a whole lot better. "Fish hook! Glad rag! Tartan biscuit!" he bellowed.

Mrs Grunt, meanwhile, simply strode across the oil-stained forecourt of Stan's Motor Repairs, past an ancient-looking petrol pump, to a pile of tyres for sale. A seagull perching on the top took one look at her determined expression and decided that the best thing to do was to make a hasty retreat. It squawked, then flapped off in a hurry.

She proceeded to lift the tyre off the top of the pile, and then took the next one in her other hand. Armed and ready for action, she returned to the hillside, took aim and threw . . .

"Weeeeeeeeeeeee!"

she cried gleefully.

The first tyre landed just ahead of the motorbike and sidecar, causing Martha – everyone assumed that the driver was Martha – to swerve. They narrowly avoided a woman on a red bike, causing *her* to swerve too. Her lemon-drop earring waggled like that dangly thing at the back of your throat.

"Sorry!" Sunny called out after her.

The lady on the bike looked back, her earring catching the light. "No worries," she said, and kept on pedalling.

The second tyre arched beautifully through the clear blue sky before knocking Martha clean off her seat and into the air, leaving the riderless motorbike to veer out of control off the cobbled street.

"POGI!" wailed Mr Grunt.

"Whoaaaaah!" wailed the POGI (which was a first).

The motorbike careered into a huge pile of hairy-roped fishing nets, the sidecar flying free, and came to an abrupt halt with an ominous judder.

There was silence but for the laughing of seagulls.

Mr Grunt turned to Mrs Grunt. "I'm proud of you, wife."

Mrs Grunt gave the biggest of yellow-and-green-teethed smiles.

Mimi was already rushing down the road towards the bike, Frizzle and Twist on course above her. Mr and Mrs Grunt were soon following as fast as their legs could carry them. Sunny went in search of the POGI.

Max's worst injury seemed to be a little whiplash, dented pride and the loss of one jet-black walrus moustache. In fact, when Mr Grunt managed to disentangle Martha from the mess of netting – where she, too, had landed – she appeared to have reclaimed it, but only when the visor of her full-face crash helmet was in the down position. It was stuck to the front.

"A strange idea for a disguise," said Officer

Needie, the island's only policeman, who'd heard the commotion from the kitchen of his tiny Police House and had rushed outside to join the excitement. He peeled the stick-on moustache off the see-through plastic. "Who should I be arresting here?"

"These two," said Mimi, indicating Max and Martha, "for attempted kidnap, along with a man called Rodders Lasenby, who we have under citizen's arrest back on our boat moored in Hydrock Cove." She thought it best not to mention Mrs Grunt's many-knotted ropes and the sock-in-the-mouth treatment.

"Did you say Rodders Lasenby?" said the policeman, looking SO excited.

"No, we said spoon-feed my antelope with

ketchup!" snapped Mrs Grunt.

Fortunately, Officer Needie appeared not to hear her. He was busy removing a notebook from his back pocket and referring to something he'd written inside. "Mr Lasenby is wanted on the mainland for everything from stealing all his shareholders' money to locking his DOM in the cellar."

"His DOM?" asked Mimi.

The young policeman referred to his notebook. "Er . . . It stands for 'Dear Old Mum', apparently," he said.

"So he wasn't joking!" Mimi gasped. "Is she OK?"

"Fine." The policeman nodded. "It says here that she managed to tunnel her way out of the cellar through the dirt floor, using only her false teeth."

"What a remarkable woman," said Mimi.

Officer Needie watched the tiny little hummingbirds hovering in a blur above her pink-bespectacled, pink-bowed head. "Quite," he said. "Would you mind helping me take these two to the island lock-up . . . ? We don't have much crime in these parts and I'm the only one on duty."

"Happy to," said Mrs Grunt. "Can I throw another tyre at them first?"

"Best not," said the policeman.

"Pity," said Mr Grunt. "The old saddlebag is an excellent shot."

Sunny, meanwhile, had found the POGI, who'd rolled some distance from his would-be kidnappers and come to rest just around the corner, past a shop selling buckets, spades and rubber rings, against a large metal bollard.

"POGI!" cried Sunny. "Are you all right?"

"POGI?" said the POGI, sounding confused.

He was lying on his side in his barrel, but managed to get to his feet. Then it happened. Hitting the bollard had damaged the barrel and one of the metal hoops fell off, causing the whole thing to fall apart, to reveal –

"JEREMY?!" said Sunny with a gasp.

And sure enough, there, right there in front of Sunny – in just a pair of snazzy red shorts

and a string vest – stood Jeremy, the little man who lived in a fibreglass tomato, who'd once kicked Mr Grunt in the shins. Very hard.

"Hello, Sunny," said Jeremy, more than a little sheepishly in his usual voice, rather than the special one he'd used to say, "POGI."

Sunny gasped. He remembered having said to Mimi that the POGI must be the size of Jeremy . . . and it had turned out to *be* him. "You're the POGI?" he said in amazement.

"No, not exactly," said the ex-circus-performer.

"So what's going on?" Sunny demanded. "Why was Dad hired to get *you* to the island?"

Jeremy looked at him and sighed.

"And why did you only ever say POGI?" Sunny added.

"If I'd said anything else, one of you might have recognised my voice," said Jeremy at last. Despite the shorts and string vest, he looked very naked without his barrel. "Do you know what a decoy is?"

Sunny had a sudden memory of a very lifelike wooden duck that Mr Grunt had once found in a pond and thrown at a passing chef, in an attempt to knock his funny-looking chef's hat off. Mr Grunt had explained that the pretend duck was a decoy duck, designed to attract other ducks, which duck-hunters would then shoot.

"You're a pretend Person Of Great Importance designed to attract the real Person Of Great Importance?" he asked.

"No, not exactly," said Jeremy, who'd now plonked himself down on the cobbles and was leaning against the bollard, pieces of broken barrel littering the ground around him, like the peel off some large, wooden fruit. "Certain people know that the POGI has to get to the island. My job is to pretend to be the POGI and to attract all the attention so the *real* POGI can reach here undetected."

"Well, it worked with Rodders Lasenby," said Sunny. "*And* Max and Martha!"

"It's been amazing," said Jeremy. "And I feel bad about it now. I don't think anyone believed that your father would succeed in getting me here in a million years!"

"You mean—"

"Everyone thought I'd have been captured a long time ago."

"Dad is going to be SO angry when he finds out," said Sunny, peering around the corner, where he could see Mr Grunt talking to the policeman. "What about this Mrs Bayliss we're going to see?"

"That's the point," said Jeremy. "There is

no Mrs Bayliss. The real POGI is making his or her way to the island, but not to see this made-up person!"

"Made-up?" asked Sunny.

The little man sighed. "News somehow leaked out that the real POGI was coming to the island for a secret meeting but by then it was too late to rearrange the meeting place. So they had to come up with a fake POGI – me – meeting a non-existent person, Mrs Bayliss, drawing the attention away—"

"– from the *real* POGI reaching the island," Sunny interrupted. "I get it, I get it. But why not have a fake Mrs Bayliss too?"

"I've already told you, Sunny." Jeremy sighed. "No one thought I'd get this far."

Just then, Officer Needie marched past holding Max by the scruff of the neck, closely followed by Mr and Mrs Grunt, who were carrying Martha sideways, like an ironing board. Mr Grunt was at the front and Mrs Grunt at the foot end.

Mr Grunt turned to look at Sunny, who quickly stood in front of the seated Jeremy.

"How's the POGI?" asked Mr Grunt.

"Fine," said Sunny.

"Good," said Mr Grunt. "We'll be back in a minute."

With Martha and Max safely locked up in the tiny island police station – their moustache returned to them by a kindly policeman – Mr Grunt decided it was time to make a speech.

He stood on an empty fish crate.

"My job was simply to safely deliver

the POGI." He paused and looked around. "Where is the POGI?" he asked.

"Gone—" began Sunny.

"– to buy cheese," Mimi added. (Sunny had quickly explained the whole POGI/Jeremy, Jeremy/POGI situation to her, before telling her his plan. This had required some frantic running around and finding of things while Mr and Mrs Grunt were with Officer Needie.)

"Shame," said Mr Grunt. "He's missing my speech."

"Not fair," muttered Mrs Grunt. "Why can't *I* miss your rotten speech?"

"What?"

"Nothing."

Mr Grunt stared at her as if she were a bag of broken biscuits, and tried again. "My job was simply to safely deliver the POGI and to keep him out of the hands of the . . . the . . ."

He tried to think of the right words.

"Handymen?" suggested Mrs Grunt. "Glove-monkeys?"

"Glove-monkeys?"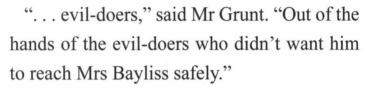

"Glove-monkeys!!!"

". . . evil-doers," said Mr Grunt. "Out of the hands of the evil-doers who didn't want him to reach Mrs Bayliss safely."

Mrs Grunt started clapping.

"I haven't finished, wife!" he hissed.

"Then get on with it!" said Mrs Grunt. "Eggnog."

One or two curious islanders had stopped to see what was going on. Mr Grunt produced a small fish from his trouser pocket and threw it at them, before continuing. "But we managed to do a whole lot more than that. Thanks to you, and Fingers and Speedy McGinty, we actually caught the—"

"Dandruff? Chickenpox?"

"Villains," said Mr Grunt. "We caught the villains. So well done, all!"

"Have you finished *now*?" asked Mrs Grunt.

"Now." Mr Grunt nodded.

She started clapping wildly.

"Now," said Mr Grunt beaming with pride, "let's find the POGI and take him to Mrs Bayliss."

The raggle-taggle group made their way back up the cobbled street, past the fishermen's cottages and Stan's Motor Repairs, where Sunny and Mimi stopped briefly to return the two borrowed tyres. (They'd been carrying one each, and they'd found them surprisingly heavy to lug up a hill.) Now they arrived at the cottage in Mr Grunt's written instructions. The one where the made-up Mrs Bayliss supposedly lived.

"Look," said Sunny, pointing to a postcard which he himself had pinned to the front door not five minutes earlier. "It's addressed to you, Dad." He pulled out the drawing pin – which Mimi had taken from the notice board outside the police station – and handed the postcard (a free one from the island's tourist information kiosk) to Mr Grunt. It read:

Dear Mr Grunt   POST CARD
Congratulations!
Mission accomplished.
I have left with Mrs.
Bayliss through a
secret tunnel so will
not see you again.
    Thank you.
    The POG I

Mr.
Grunt

Mr Grunt wiped the corner of his eye with a very grubby sleeve. He sniffed. "That's nice," he said. "Truth be told, I grew rather fond of the little fellow."

"How do we know that it's from him?" Mrs Grunt demanded.

Mimi shot Sunny a worried look.

"Whatcha mean, wife?" demanded Mr Grunt.

"What if the note was actually written by one of them glove-monkeys?"

"HA!" said Mr Grunt (and about time too). "I can tell it was written by the POGI because it was pinned on the door at POGI height. Because it is written in teeny-weeny ankle-snapping handwriting and the POGI is tiny. And . . ." Mr Grunt trailed off. He appeared to have run out of ideas.

"And what?" said Mrs Grunt.

"And it's *signed* by him," said Sunny, pointing at the signature.

"Precisely!" said Mr Grunt. "It says 'The POGI' at the bottom."

"Good point, husband," said Mrs Grunt. "I really can be stupid sometimes."

Mr Grunt didn't disagree with that (except perhaps for the "sometimes" part).

Mimi and Sunny sighed with relief.

Chapter Fifteen
The Final Chapter

Speedy McGinty was happy to captain *The Merry Dance* on its return voyage and, with Rodders Lasenby now crammed into the island's one holding cell with Max and Martha – whose real names later turned out to be Michael and Mandy Jinx – it was no one but friends and family on board. And more family than Sunny had bargained for.

The penny finally dropped when he was bringing Speedy McGinty a snack in the wheelhouse on their second day back at sea.

"I've just realised why you look so familiar!" said Sunny. "I don't know why I didn't see it before."

"You saw my picture in a magazine, perhaps?" she said.

Sunny handed her a plate – a real plate, not a hubcap – with a sandwich on it.

"Thank you," she said cautiously, taking it with one hand while keeping the other on the wheel. She eyed the snack suspiciously.

"It's OK," said Sunny with a grin. "It's cheese. I made it with the remains of the POGI's cheese supplies he left behind."

Jeremy had decided to stay on the island

until his attempted kidnappers came to court. He fancied some sun and sand. It got very stuffy living in a windowless fibreglass fruit.

"Thank you," said Speedy McGinty again. And this time she meant it.

"You have Dad's eyes," said Sunny. "They're the same unusual colour!"

Speedy McGinty stared down at her plate. She wouldn't meet his gaze.

"There's a strong . . . what's the phrase? Family resemblance. You and Dad are related, aren't you? *That's* why you care so much for his safety. That's why you came to warn us in your plane."

Speedy McGinty looked at the boy for a while and said nothing. Eventually, she spoke. "Yes," she said. "We're brother and sister."

"Wow," said Sunny. "Wow." He looked out of the window at the horizon. Nothing but sea and sky. Then another thought struck him. "He doesn't know, does he?" he said.

"No," said Speedy McGinty at last. "When we were kids, I was sent away for treatment for these legs of mine, but I ended up staying. I grew up there and married the most handsome man I've ever seen in my life, before or since: Johnson McGinty." She stared up at the roof of the wheelhouse, but that wasn't what she saw in her mind's eye. "He was the finest soup salesman in the West. Won the Golden Ladle eight years in a row. I kept his name even after he died – it was an accident between two tanker trucks, one carrying pea and ham and the other carrying mulligatawny – and I finally came to live back here . . ."

"Then one day Dad turns up and tries to steal your door knocker and you realised who it was," said Sunny. His eyes glistened.

"Recognised him at once, though he didn't recognise me," said Speedy. "As odd lookin' as ever. That's my Cankle, I thought. And I was right. I didn't tell him who I was, though.

Too much time passed. Too much water under the bridge."

"Wow," said Sunny (for the third time). Then he grinned. "Dad's name is Cankle?"

"Sure is," said Speedy McGinty. "Cankle Grunt."

"That's cool," said Sunny. "What's yours?"

Speedy McGinty fixed his eyes with hers. "My name," she said, "is Speedy McGinty, wife of the late, much missed Johnson McGinty. Got that, Sunny?"

"Got it," said Sunny.

"Got what?" asked Mrs Grunt, bursting through the door. "Smallpox? Bedbugs? Time on your hands?"

"HA!" said Mr Grunt from the deck. "Come and feed that elephant of yours, will you, Sunny? He's giving me the hungry look."

"On my way," said Sunny. He sighed, but

inside he felt strangely happy.

A few days later, when they arrived back at Isaac's Port, Ma Brackenbury came out of her sentry-like box to greet them. Speedy McGinty – who, between you and me, was born Miss Kitty Grunt – made steering *The Merry Dance* into the harbour look easy. Hawsers were thrown and in next to no time the boat was safely moored in place.

(OK, OK, so you're wondering why Mr Grunt had the strange name Cankle while his sister was simply called Kitty. The answer is simple: *Old* Mr Grunt got to name their boy Cankle, while it was his wife who named their girl Kitty. See? Obvious.)

"Where's the man in the fancy uniform?" asked Ma Brackenbury when she saw someone else was piloting the boat.

"Jail," said Mimi. "Or he soon will be."

Ma Brackenbury cackled. "Good," she said. "I'll bet it was him who had old Captain Haunch nobbled, so's he could take his place on your boat." She banged her scrimshaw-headed walking stick on the harbour wall with a clack.

"Nobbled?" asked Sunny.

"Someone slipped something into his drink," said Ma Brackenbury. She still had the empty, long-stemmed clay pipe between her teeth and noisily sucked in air. "He fell down the stairs then slept like a baby for two days, he did. Woke up with a headache as bad as the smell of a merman's armpit."

"And that's bad?" said Mimi.

"Terrrible," said Ma Brackenbury, making the word sound like it had three "r"s in it. (Go on. You can count them.)

Mr Grunt managed to climb up the iron rungs of an inner harbour ladder while carrying Speedy McGinty, which is easier said than done. Fortunately the tide was high, so the climb was a short one.

Fingers reached up with his trunk from the deck of the boat and placed the folded wheelchair on the harbour wall.

Mimi unfolded it and wheeled it into position. Mr Grunt placed Speedy in it. "Thanks," she said.

"Thank YOU," said Mr Grunt. "We'd never have got the POGI to the island if it weren't for you."

Mrs Grunt didn't like not being the centre of her husband's attention, so chose to change the subject by pushing a passing fisherman off the harbour wall into the sea.

There was a terrible SPLASH!

"Sorry," she said. "I couldn't help myself."
She gave what she thought was a girlish giggle
(which was *not* a pretty sound).

"You all right?" Ma Brackenbury called out.

"Yur, fine," called out the sodden fisherman,
clambering back on to the wall.

Once Fingers, Clip and Clop and the caravan
were back on dry land, with more than a little
help from a number of Isaac's Port's fishermen
– including Wellum and Mollusc, of course –
it was time to head back to Bigg Manor, via
Hutton's Vale, to drop off Speedy McGinty at

her bungalow.

Ma Brackenbury made them clear a couple of elephant-dung pancakes off the harbour wall before they went, so add them to the Official Dung Count, if you're keeping score.

"Do you reckon the *real* POGI made it safely to the island?" Mimi asked Sunny, sitting beside him up on Fingers' back, as the elephant pulled the caravan behind him.

"With everyone's eyes on our POGI, I bet she did," he said.

"She?" said Mimi.

"It was something Jeremy said," Sunny explained. "He described the POGI making his or *her* way to the

island . . . and that got me wondering."

"About what?"

"About a woman we ran into more than once along the way." He looked at one of the orange plastic floats, dangling from a tangle of fishnets, and smiled.

Stories can, of course, end where you want them to end and I could easily end this one here. But, for me, this tale wasn't really complete until Mr and Mrs Grunt were back where they started: with Old Mr Grunt in the grounds of Bigg Manor.

"Welcome home, son," said Old Mr Grunt. He sounded bunged up because he had a finger in his nose, up to the knuckle. "Made you a present."

"A present, Da?" said Mr Grunt.

"For your birthday, lad." He thrust a parcel

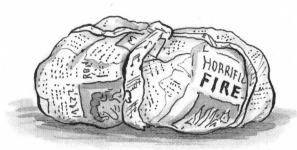

into Mr Grunt's hand.

The wrapping paper was old newspaper. Sunny could clearly read the headline: HORRIFIC FIRE.

What a lovely birthday message, he thought.

The "ribbon" was made from an old, thin, rat-chewed tie, covered in musical notes. Mr Grunt pulled one end to undo the bow.

"Beautifully wrapped," he said.

"I wish you went to this much trouble for *my* birthday," said Mrs Grunt.

"You're too old for birthdays," said Mr Grunt.

"Younger than you," said Mrs Grunt.

"You don't look it."

"Do."

"Don't."

"Do."

"Wrinkle-bucket!" said Mr Grunt.

Mrs Grunt picked up a small log and threw it at him. He ducked and it narrowly missed Frizzle and Twist.

"Sorry, Moomoo," said Mrs Grunt.

"Mimi," said Mimi.

"Quiet," said Mr Grunt. "Don't spoil the moment."

He tore off the last of the newspaper to reveal a long, thin, knitted thing, which he proceeded to wind round his neck, throwing one end over his shoulder.

"Lovely scarf, Da!" he said.

There was a moment's silence.

The calm before the storm . . .

Old Mr Grunt's howl of rage could be heard

in the furthest reaches of the ruinous Bigg Manor. Sunny and Mimi dived for cover

behind a conveniently placed – and very familiar – stone wall.

"Ooof!" said Sunny. He turned to Mimi, sprawled on the grass beside him, and smiled.

Adventures were all very well, but it was *good* to be home.